—

Green Heart

Green Heart

TWO NOVELS:

Green Angel and *Green Witch*

ALICE HOFFMAN

Scholastic Inc.

NEW YORK TORONTO LONDON AUCKLAND
SYDNEY MEXICO CITY NEW DELHI HONG KONG

Green Angel was originally published in hardcover by Scholastic Press in 2003. *Green Witch* was originally published in hardcover by Scholastic Press in 2010.   ISBN 978-0-545-14196-3. All rights reserved. Published by Scholastic Inc.

For information regarding

permission, write to Scholastic Inc.,

Attention: Permissions Department,

557 Broadway, New York, NY

10012.

by Matt Mahurin. Green Witch. ISBN 978-0-545-14195-6 Text Copyright © 2010 by Alice Hoffman.

12 11 10 9 8 7 6 5 4 3 2 1   11 12 13 14 15 16/0 · Printed in the U.S.A.   40

The text type was set in Adobe Garamond. · Book design by Elizabeth B. Parisi.

Green Angel

Green Angel

ALICE HOFFMAN

Green Angel

Heart

This is how it happened

I once believed that life was a gift. I thought whatever I wanted I would someday possess. Is that greed, or only youth? Is it hope or stupidity? As far as I was concerned the future was a book I could write to suit myself, chapter after chapter of good fortune. All was right with the world, and my place in it was assured, or so I thought then. I had no idea that all stories unfold like white flowers, petal by petal, each in its own time and season, dependent on circumstance and fate. The future is something no one can foretell.

My family had always lived on the ridgetop above the village in a county where days were sunny and warm. At twilight, dusk wove across the meadows like a dream of the next day to come. People said we were blessed, and maybe that was true. My father was honest and strong. My mother collected blue jay feathers, preferring them to her pearls. My little sister, Aurora, was as wild as she was beautiful. Aurora could climb a tree in the blink of an eye. She could disappear into the woods like moonlight. She could dance for hours and never tire.

I was the least among them, nothing special, just a girl. I was a moody, dark weed; still, they called me Green because of my talents in the garden. My mother was the one who taught me everything I knew — to bury old boots beneath peach trees to ensure they'll bear the sweetest fruit, to douse roses with vinegar-water to chase away beetles, to plant when the moon wanes and harvest when it is on the rise.

My sister, Aurora, could never sit still and pay attention. She chased after frogs, she trailed her prettiest dresses through the mud, she stole apples from our neighbor's orchard, she laughed so hard whenever her snappy little terrier, Onion, danced on his hind legs, we thought she'd never come to her senses. Aurora didn't listen to a word my mother said. We all knew she couldn't stay in one place any longer than moonlight could. Every time she ran through the garden the warblers and sparrows would follow her. Bees would drink the sweat from her skin and never once sting. My mother laughed and said the honey in our hives would taste especially wild and sweet.

At night, Aurora and I shared a room. Aurora slept without blankets or pillows, her pale hair streaming. Once or twice I had awoken to spy her curled up on the floor with her little dog. As she dreamed, white moths hovered above her, more drawn to her than they were to the moon or to the lantern my father kept on the porch, a beacon that signaled to anyone who might lose his way in the woods.

Aurora was made out of laughter and moonlight, but I was nothing like that. Unlike my fearless sister, I was afraid of blackbirds and thunder. I couldn't get a good night's sleep unless I had three feather pillows under my head and two down quilts covering me. But I was the one who could sit in the garden for hours, unmoving, as I watched seedlings unfold. I was Green, with my long, dark hair and my endless patience. A weed who grew too tall. I was Green, who never smiled at anyone, who preferred roses and asparagus to people. I was shy and ill at ease, uncomfortable with girls my own age, unwilling to talk to the boys at school. I wasn't good company, that was true, and people avoided me, but that was all right. I was too busy dreaming.

My head was in the clouds even on the days we went into town. I didn't notice when people said hello to me. I was too busy thinking about the future to come. When my mother sent us to do her shopping, I was too timid to enter the market and sent my sister in my place.

Aurora laughed at how fainthearted I was.

They won't bite you, she said.

All the same, I kept my distance. I didn't mind if the storekeepers favored my sister. They gave her sweets, mints and sugared almonds, which she would share evenly, fifty-fifty. Aurora always remembered me. I was a reflection of what she was, a dark pond to mirror her moonlight. I hugged her, grateful that she didn't notice I was less than she was. I ran home with her through the woods even though she was faster and more graceful than I would ever be. I didn't care who preferred my good-natured sister. I was Green, who was more comfortable in shadows. Green, who faded in the light of my sister. How could I not defer to her? The moon itself paled compared to her. Even the white moths would rather circle around her than fly into the sky up above.

But I knew how to listen. I was the one who paid attention to the lessons my mother taught us.

I learned that the roots of the foxglove were poisonous, that verbena could quiet headaches, that quince could be boiled into a sticky, delicious jam. In time, I knew more than my mother. Soon, she began to turn to me for advice. When should we harvest? When should we sow? What would do best in the patch of sunlight beside the gate?

I could whisper to the old, twisted wisteria and it would turn green at my urging. I could encourage the sweet peas to blossom with one word. Let Aurora smile at the shopkeepers and wave to the boys in the school yard. My dreams were of night-blooming flowers, white on the outside, but green as my heart on the inside, green as my garden grew.

I never complained when people didn't notice me. I was certain my time would come soon enough. There was dirt under my fingernails and I was too shy to speak, but on my next birthday I would turn sixteen. Everything would change then. I would cast away my fears and step into my future. I would comb the tangles from my hair and wash the dirt away. When I walked through town, people would whisper, *Is that Green?* And I would say, *Yes it's me, I've been here all along, but you've been too blind to see.*

I would have gone with my family on the day that it happened, but someone had to stay home and pull weeds. Someone had to coax the tomatoes into turning red and persuade the squash blossoms to bloom, and that person was me. We lived within sight of the city, which glowed silver at night and shone like gold in the afternoon. Every week we brought our vegetables across the river to sell to city people who couldn't get enough of our peas and lettuce and beans. Every week we crossed the bridge, and as we did I held my breath. I could feel happiness then.

I lived for those trips to the city. On the weeks I couldn't go, I pouted for hours. The city was my treasure, and I loved everything about it: the shops on the avenues, the books in the stalls, the chocolates weighed and measured by vendors in the streets. No one in the city cared if your hair was long and tangled, or if there was dirt under your fingernails. No one cared if you whispered a greeting to the linden trees that circled the park where we set up our stand. You could be who you wanted to be in the city. You could be whoever you were deep inside. It was like a garden of people, the only place where I didn't feel alone in a crowd.

Naturally, I wanted to go that day. It was my turn. But Aurora was still too young to stay by herself. And on this trip my father was needed to carry the heavy crates, wooden boxes overflowing from the best harvest we'd had in years. As for my mother, she was the one who drew the customers, like the white moths who were entranced by Aurora. People on the street couldn't resist my mother's sweet voice, her gentle hands, her long, black hair, raven-colored, like mine. It was clear she couldn't stay.

It made sense for me to work in the garden, for me to be the one who stayed home, but I was angry all the same. When my family set out to leave, they called good-bye, but I didn't answer. My father whistled a tune, and although the sparrows returned his call I did not. I wouldn't even look at him, even though he was so strong and so kind. I didn't say a word.

I'll bring you something special, Aurora promised. I knew she'd spend all her free time searching for a gift that would please me, a book or a bag of sweets, but I didn't blow her a kiss or wish her well.

There will be plenty of times for you to be the one to go, my mother told me. My mother, who was so beautiful, who knew the secrets of the growing season, who always assured me that everyone had her own path, and that mine could be found in the garden.

Green, my mother said to me that day, moments before they left for the city, *we're leaving you behind because you're the one who's needed most of all.*

Now that she was standing next to me, I was surprised to find that I was almost as tall as my mother. I felt my love for her in the back of my throat, like a stone, heavy, making it impossible for me to speak. I was almost a woman myself. Too old to admit I was wrong, or so I thought then. Too old to race after my mother when she turned to leave. I had too much pride to say good-bye. I kept my nose in the air and my back to them. I was Green, moody and prideful and angry.

I will forever remember that I turned away.

We had so many birds in the trees back then, and each one sang to me while I did my work. I weeded for hours, until my hands ached. Three blue jay feathers drifted down to me. I kept them in my pocket as a gift for my mother, if I decided to forgive her.

The day was perfect, cloudless and blue; still I continued to feel sorry for myself. At noon, I decided to take my lunch up to the hillside that overlooked the city. I let my sister's dog, Onion, trail after me even though he was an annoying beggar who sometimes growled when he saw me. Today Onion tolerated me because my sister wasn't there, but I knew I was just a substitute for Aurora.

It was so warm that I was tired by the time I reached the top of the hill. I can remember the way it felt to breathe in the hot, still air. The stitch in my side. The river in the distance, flat as a mirror. The brambles that had caught in my long, black hair. The blue jays' feathers in my pocket. The chattering of a wood thrush overhead. The dog whining softly. The pulse in my throat at the last moment of the world as it was.

People who were close by said they could see people jumping from the buildings, like silver birds, like bright diamonds. The ground shook, people said, but from where I stood all I could see was smoke. I could hear the whoosh of the fire all these miles away, across the river, past the woods. I could hear it as if it were happening inside my own head.

I ran down the hill so fast, my clothes were torn to shreds on the brambles. My heart was in my mouth. I thought of my mother, measuring out green beans on a scale with her gentle hands. I thought of my father, who could whistle so many tunes with such sweetness, every variety of bird in our garden would answer. I thought of my sister, whose hair was white as snow, the wild girl who never stopped to listen, always the opposite of me. My sister, who was as familiar as the moon up above, changeable, yes, but always there for me to depend upon.

Ashes had swept across the river in black whirl-winds. I ran to escape them, through the yard, into the house. But there was no escape. Embers flew in through the open windows and set the ends of my hair on fire. I wrapped a wet towel around my head. Steam rose in billows from beneath the towel and I smelled like smoke. But worst of all, the embers had flown into my eyes. My eyes burned so badly, I grew dizzy with the pain.

My sister's little dog had followed me home. He knew something was wrong and now he barked at the sky, the world, the open door, which

I ran to slam shut as I tried to stop the flow of embers. I fastened the bolt, then held my hands over my ears. I didn't want to hear the roar of the fire, so far away, across the river. I wanted silence, peace, blue skies, yesterday. But no matter what, I could hear it still. No matter what, it was burning.

I crawled under the dining room table, smelling like smoke and half-blinded by cinders. Little bits of hot embers flew under the door. Onion followed and lay shivering in my lap. I was Green, who was too shy to speak. Green, too angry to say good-bye. Green, who was always waiting for the future, biding her time. Now the future was here and the silver city across the river was on fire and I was hiding under the table, where I stayed until darkness fell.

After a while I couldn't hear the fire anymore. The dog whimpered, but I hushed him. I could barely see, but my ears were good. I was the one who could hear the wisteria unfolding. I could hear the sweet peas climbing the fence, the asparagus rising through the soil. Now, I was listening harder than ever. I was waiting for my family to come home. All they had to do was run from the fire. All they needed was to cross the river. Swim, if they must. Crawl, if need be. Find their way home in the dark, in the whirlwinds, in the burning embers. Surely they would appear if only I waited long enough. I was patient Green, after all. Green, who knew how to listen.

They were in the city for only a single day. Luck couldn't be as bad as that, could it? Was that the way the future worked? Unknowable, unchangeable, always uncertain. They might have gone to the city the day before or the day after. They might have been stopped by the rising of the drawbridge, by a bee sting, by a sudden storm. They might have not gone at all.

But they were there when it happened. And I was not.

It was days before I stopped listening for them, my mother's footsteps, my father's whistle, my sister's wild laughter. I had already decided that I would not allow myself to cry until they came home safely. Tears now would be an admission that they were gone. That I could stop listening. I wasn't ready for that.

Every morning I rose from my fitful sleep in the bed I'd made beneath the table expecting to find a trail of my family's footsteps on our dusty floor. I would embrace them and tell them how much I loved them. I would tell them that I'd meant to hug them and kiss them good-bye. Only then would I let the tears wash over my burning eyes.

But the days wore on and I heard nothing. Dark, fiery days that were silent as stone. No one came home. No one called out my name. Finally, I went to open the door. I could smell burning metal. I could see sparks in the trees, drifting like fireflies. All of those white pages on which I had planned to write my future were burning around the edges, first red, then black, then blue with flame.

My sister's dog refused to step past the threshold. He peed in a corner; he trembled and howled. Poor Onion was missing Aurora. His howls were like mourning cries. I couldn't listen to him, so I went outside and looked up at the black sky. My eyes were still burning, my vision was blurry, but even I could tell there were no stars. Ashes were falling down, a soft black rain. The white moths had dropped from above; they'd scattered like leaves, lining the stone path to our door, gleaming like black opals.

I found my way back to the top of the hill. There was only a handful of silver on the other side of the river now. Pale beacons, pale light. I thought about how time had always stretched out before me, those white empty pages that were mine alone. I thought about how hot it had been at the moment when it happened. How everything around me had been green as far as the eye could see. How the sky had been so cloudless, not even a puff of white.

As I walked back to my house in the dark, making my way past the brambles, I noticed that the songbirds who were usually asleep in their nests at this hour were fluttering nervously from tree to tree. It was then I realized it wasn't nighttime at all, but sooty daylight, noon perhaps. The sun had been shadowed by ashes. Now I understood. The world as I knew it was gone forever. What I had thought was the moon up above, as familiar as Aurora's face, was in fact the cloudy sun. On this day, even that circle of light looked so much smaller than it once had, a teardrop in the sky.

People in town must have assumed I had perished along with my family. No one came to search for me, and that was just as well. I was glad to be deep in the woods, away from them all. If anyone had tried to rescue me, I would have hidden behind our barn. I would have gone to the darkest part of the woods where the hedges were ten feet tall and the brambles cut the soles of your feet right through your shoes.

My grief was cold. It was nothing to share. It was nothing to speak about, nothing to feel.

I ate food from the pantry and kicked at the ashes in the garden. But I was lazy and did no work. What was the point? If this was the future, I wasn't certain I wanted to be in it. I started to feel as though I were disappearing. Perhaps I myself was a figment of my own imagination, a storm cloud, a wisp of smoke, a burning ember.

I could hear people singing in town; I could hear the church bells ringing. People were going about the business of living as best they could. They could see past today, into tomorrow. But not me. Grief had tied me in knots. There was no gas for the stove, but I didn't cut wood. There was no tap water, but I didn't go to the well. If I could have stopped breathing, I would have. I watched time moving, slowly, like dust motes, like gnats on a summer day, circling close, but never touching me.

I was so quiet and the house was so dark that anyone coming to call would have guessed there was no one at home. The looters who came must have assumed they had the freedom to do whatever they pleased. What I had was theirs for the taking. What I had was up for grabs.

As it turned out, I didn't hear a thing until they

were inside the gate. I was deeply asleep. I had fallen into sleep the way stones fall into a well. The looters had stumbled onto the property in the middle of the night and they didn't even pretend stealth. When I heard them shouting and screaming inside of my dreams, I awoke with a start, a cold band across my chest. The dog was whimpering, but thankfully he didn't bark. Silence was what we needed. Silence was all we had while they stole everything worth taking from the garden.

I crawled to the window and saw there were maybe a dozen boys and girls my age. They strode over the delicate seedlings with heavy boots, they pawed through the piles of ash I had planned to rake in their frantic search for anything to eat. They tossed lettuce and cucumbers and squash blossoms into the wheelbarrow they'd stolen from our barn. Whatever they didn't gorge on was loaded onto the wheelbarrow, till it nearly overflowed. Blackened peppers, singed peas, burnt cauliflower, all of it ripped from the garden. All of it gone before I could count to three.

I was quiet because I could tell they'd been drinking. There was the edge of something dark out there in the garden as they tugged and pulled at everything I had worked so hard to grow. Fights broke out. Words were slurred. I recognized a girl named Heather Jones I'd been at school with along with several boys from my classes. I thought perhaps they had also lost their families. I knew Heather's parents worked in the city. I knew they'd never let her run wild with a greedy horde such as this.

No one out in the garden looked like themselves in the black ashy night. The boys had painted their faces with mud and berry juice. The girls were all barefoot, in spite of the fact that there were still burning embers at the bottom of the piles of ashes. I had canned food in the pantry, maybe enough to share, but these intruders looked desperate. They wanted to take whatever they saw, they wanted to ruin anything that thwarted them, and the most I could do was crouch by the window and watch them. I was Green, who stayed in the shadows, who shivered and hushed the dog when it whimpered as the looters wrecked fences, tore out stakes, danced in the ashes. Green, who did nothing but shake while the troop in the yard destroyed everything in their path.

Perhaps they would have come into the house after that and taken whatever they wanted. Perhaps that was why one of the boys started up the path littered with fallen white moths. But a stone hit that boy square in the back, startling him. He stopped and turned to the woods. Something hooted out there. There was a cackle, human or animal — it was impossible to tell.

Afraid? several in the crowd called when he noticed the other boy had stopped on the path to our house.

More stones fell then, one after another. The cackle rose high, a hen, a ghost, a spirit, the wind. No one knew what it was, but the mob was not about to wait and find out.

Heather Jones ran away first, crying that there was even worse luck in store for those who stayed where they were. There should have been strength in numbers, but once the looters stopped wrecking things they were only boys and girls, easily frightened. The rest of the crowd soon followed Heather. Why shouldn't they go? They had already taken everything edible, piled into the wheelbarrow. They'd already had their fun.

When I went out in the morning, there was nothing left but ashes and stones. We had been at the height of our harvest, row after row of new zucchini and purple onions, of peppers that were shiny as frogs and blueberry bushes that were thickening with fruit. That garden was gone. Those days were over. Standing there, I knew my family wasn't coming back. I could feel it the way you can feel the wind across your face. Invisible, but certain. Sure as the blood in your veins.

I carried the stones, which had chased the looters from our garden, in all of my pockets. I took them far into the woods, out to where the oldest trees grew. Was it an accident that these stones had fallen, or was it something more? Should I be grateful to someone who had watched over me? I didn't know what to believe. I didn't know if I believed in anything at all.

Carefully, I made three piles: one for my mother, one for my father, one for my little sister. Every day I carted stones and every day I added to the growing stacks. Black for my mother, silver for my father, pure white for my sister, the hardest to find. The white stones tossed into our garden were best of all, they were like moonstones, aglow with light.

Wherever I went, I carried stones in my pockets, my hands, my boots. It was my duty, my burden, my gift, my soul, the reason I woke in the morning and went to sleep at night. Now I had a purpose, to build the stone stacks. I had known the woods before, now I knew them nearly blind and in the dark. I could find my way by touch. My fingers could tell the difference between east and west. I could rub a clod of dirt under my thumb and gauge how close to the river I was. Before long, I could hold a fallen feather in the palm of my hand

and tell whether it belonged to a jay or a sparrow or a dove.

When the stacks of stones were tall as the tallest men in the village, I went on to my next task. I began to clean the house. I was determined to get rid of all the ashes. I swept the floor until the straw bristles of the broom were ragged from use. I cleaned until my fingers hurt, and when it was done, when the brass doorknobs were shining and the kettles were scrubbed and the windows were bright with light, I turned on myself.

I chopped off all my burnt hair with the scissors my mother had used to trim the roses beside the front door. My hair was nothing more than a black curtain. I didn't need it anymore. My hair reminded me of my mother, it was the only way I was like her, the one feature we shared. I didn't want to be prideful anymore. I wanted to be as hard and brittle as the stones I carted into the woods, stones that could not feel or cry or see. That is what I wished for as I walked past the brambles, as I built the stacks in the woods higher and higher. I wished not to feel anything at all.

I had no idea that even in the darkest world, there are some wishes that can come true. Now I understand that those are the ones to think over most carefully. Those are the wishes that can wound just as surely as the sharpest arrow.

In no time, what I wished for, I became.

Soon enough, I began wearing my father's old black boots and a battered leather jacket that felt like armor. I kept several smooth rocks in my pockets along with a slingshot fashioned out of wood and a belt. I planned to be ready in case the looters came back. I smoked cigarettes I discovered in a drawer. I drank from the bottle of gin kept in the cupboard until my stomach burned. One night when the sky was ash-colored, I went into the ruined garden and clipped the thorns from the bare rosebushes, then sewed them to my clothes, one by one, until my fingers bled. Now I was ready to feel nothing. I was protected from feeling anything at all.

All the same, there was less and less food in the pantry and my stomach growled all the time. I hated it for wanting food. I didn't deserve anything, not food to ease my hunger or water to ease my thirst. I should have been on that street weighing vegetables when it happened. Instead, I had been weeding and thinking about my lunch. I was standing under the perfect, blue sky feeling sorry for myself.

That was when I took a pin and some black ink. I began to mark my arm. I outlined a raven, and then a bat, then a rose that looked like a flower found at the end of the world. That's who I was now without my mother and my father and my moonlit sister. Blood and ink. Darkness where before there had been patience, black where there'd once been green.

The decision of who would stay and who would go to the city was made arbitrarily that day, a single white page of fate that altered our future.

I could have insisted. I could have run after them. Then I would have been there to turn to my mother at the instant when it happened. The last thing I saw would have been her black hair and the fire behind her, red as roses.

But I was the one who was still alive, the girl whose eyes burned, whose vision was blurry, whose stomach growled, who wrote upon herself with black ink, as if that could change anything. Once, I had wanted only one thing: to be sixteen. One simple, easy desire. That day wasn't so far away, but it might as well have been forever. I was no more certain that my wish would be granted than I was that daylight would remain, that the birds would sing, that my garden would grow.

Soul

This is what I dreamed

Wanting only darkness, I began to sleep. I slept longer and longer. I ignored daylight and hope. I didn't care if the sky had begun to clear. Most of the ashes had fallen to the ground, leaving the horizon a faint washed-out blue. On several occasions I had noticed white clouds. There was the promise of sunshine. That wasn't what I wanted. I would rather sleep than eat or see the sky. Each time I put away my ink and pins, I closed all the windows. I drew the shades. When I went to sleep, under the table where I felt safer, I tied a scarf around my burning eyes so not even the tiniest bit of light could disturb me or remind me of what I had lost.

When I slept, I dreamed of the world as it was. My sister was clearing away the ashes. My sister was opening the window. Her hair was the color of moonlight, ice-colored, knotted from sleep.

Help me, she'd demand when the window stuck fast in my dreams, when the door wouldn't open, when the ashes were so deep she'd never be able to clear them away all alone.

I'd rise from my bed and do as she asked because I couldn't deny her anything. Once again, I was Green, who had patience. I was the girl with long, black hair who held the open book, white pages, empty and clean, black words flying like ravens, still waiting for the future, still hopeful, still me.

Whenever I dreamed and my sister was beside me, I could breathe easier. Aurora's skin was silver, aglow with light. Sometimes in my dreams she had grown up and was my age exactly. Even as my twin she was still my beloved opposite: the moon, not brackish green water. Bright, not dim. Wild, not plodding and shy. She was my sister and she knew my thoughts before they were spoken. She knew why I couldn't bear to see. Why I wanted the cinders in my eyes. Why I never bothered going to my mother's medicine cabinet, where there were so many ointments and cures. My vision was little more than shadows, but even in my dreams, I wouldn't search for a cure.

You know what you have to do in order to see, Aurora told me. She pinched me and pulled my hair to try to make me cry, but I wouldn't. Not in my sleep nor in my waking life.

My sister may have been cold as silver in my dreams, but she was as real to me as the candlesticks on the dining room table. As real as the moon climbing into the ink-black sky. As real as needles and pins. Each time I awoke, I felt her slip through my grasp, a cloud of mist evaporating in the light of day. If I couldn't see, if I shut out what was there before me and sleepwalked through my life, then I could go on dreaming. While I was sweeping the floor, while I collected buckets of water from the well, while I counted the jars of blackberry jam that were left in the pantry, first four, then two, then none at all, I was still with my sister.

Each night, before I slept, I took the black ink and tattooed ravens and roses and bats that could fly through the dark. Though I was almost blind, I could see well enough to do this. I could spy black ink, sorrow, loss, hearts breaking. I could see well enough to see that I was alone. I could see that soon enough I'd be starving if I didn't figure out what to do next.

I had picked all the blackberries that grew in the woods, all the blueberries, all the raspberries. I had found wild asparagus and made soups in the black pot I kept on the fire I left burning in the stove. My hands were rough from chopping wood, from gathering asparagus in the marshes, from collecting the few berries that hadn't been singed black from the heat across the river. There were very few tins left in the pantry, no flour, no salt. And my stomach went on growling, wanting me to stay alive.

I decided to go into town. But I wasn't a fool. I took precautions. I wore my leather jacket, my clothes with thorns, my heavy boots into which I had hammered half a dozen nails. I carried my stones and my slingshot. I was ready for looters, wild men, highway robbers. I expected almost anything, but when I left the woods for the main thorough-fare, all that greeted me was an unnatural silence.

There used to be traffic; there were trains that ran on the hour racing across the silver bridge into the city. Now the bridge had all but melted in the heat from the city. It was closed, a thick rope tied across the entrance. People stayed close to home, worried about what might await them on the open road. There used to be children headed to the river to swim on hot days; now there was no one. There used to be bicyclists, carts, farmers on their way into town to the monthly market; now there was nothing but the dust I kicked into the air with every step I took.

My sister's dog had followed me. He snarled at the few strays lurking about, pets left to fend for themselves when their owners failed to return home. On one corner there were two dead ravens, their feathers thick with ash. The plum trees that had lined the road were leafless, the bark gray. When I passed the church just outside the village, there was a sign printed with the names of everyone who'd been lost. One after another, mothers and fathers, sons and daughters. I was amazed by how many there were. But I was not surprised to see my name among them.

The girl I had been, the one called Green, they were right about her. She was gone.

The shopkeeper at the general store stared hard when he saw me. He didn't know who I was, with my short hair and my black ink and the nails in my shoes. He reached for the club he kept near his money box, ready to fight me off if need be. Even after I told him I was my parents' daughter, he didn't seem to believe me. He spoke to me from a distance, keeping the counter between us, as if he were conversing with a ghost.

Everyone said you were dead, he insisted.

I didn't dispute this. I didn't say these people were wrong. I just took what I'd brought to trade out of my backpack and held it up to the light.

The shopkeeper noticed my cloudy eyes; he could tell I was half-blind, and perhaps this was why he tried to cheat me. He told me the ring I had was copper. But I knew it was gold. My mother had kept this ring in a bowl on her dresser, and I had played with it ever since I was a baby. I knew what I held in my hands. Pure sunlight. Pure gold.

I laughed at the idea that my mother's most valued piece of jewelry was copper. The sound of my voice frightened the shopkeeper and he stepped even farther away. He didn't know what to expect from me, but one thing was certain. I wasn't shy anymore. I wasn't that quiet, moody girl Green, whom anyone could fool.

I was the girl who could touch the earth and gauge where to find the river. I was the one who could feel sorrow in the wind. I knew that gold was heavy, copper warm, and the silver candlesticks I brought forth from my backpack felt like ice.

I suppose you're going to tell me these are a deer's antlers, I said of the candlesticks, which had been cast by one of the finest silversmiths in the city. *I know what I have,* I told the shopkeeper. *I expect to be paid well.*

That was the last of any arguments at the general store. As a matter of fact, the shopkeeper called for his wife, who came to watch me with narrowed eyes, as if I were a circus act or a charlatan.

Green, the shopkeeper's wife said uncertainly. She'd known my family quite well and had often bought vegetables from my mother. But in the world we now lived in, why should she trust me any more than I trusted her? Why shouldn't she gawk at the nails in my boots, the slingshot in my pocket?

The shopkeeper and his wife tested my ability to distinguish by touch. If I could identify silver and gold, what else might I know? Sure enough I could tell green tea from black, navy beans from kidney beans, earth from ashes, honesty from deceit. I had another talent, it seemed. One that made people nervous.

After that, rumors flew around quickly enough. There were those who swore that anyone who touched my hand would be visited by bad fortune. I didn't disagree. I wanted the looters to hear about how I could turn the luck of anyone who came near me. And who was to say I wasn't cursed? I had lost my mother and my father and my sister, and sometimes when I caught a glimpse of myself in a shop window, I wondered if perhaps I hadn't lost myself as well. Every time I tried to say my name out loud the word stuck in my throat, a black stone, a silver stone, a stone as white as moonlight.

Before long, every shopkeeper on Main Street knew of my talents and my cloudy eyes. Even the looters, gathered under bridges and on street corners, were wary and stayed clear. In every store, people I'd known all my life hurried when I came to trade what I no longer desired for what I needed. They were forced to be honest with me, and they gave me what I'd come for. Gold and silver in exchange for cranberry juice, white rice, bandages, brown sugar, salt, vitamins. Coins and candlesticks for eggs, tins of baked beans, sugar, vinegar, laundry soap, candles.

There were good people in town who were helping out their neighbors and others who saw an opportunity for greed. Some people were busy cleaning the ashes out of the schoolhouse, while others were selling overpriced lanterns and oil and counting their profits. Honorable or not, most people were desperate for good fortune. Many hung horseshoes above their doors. They made certain to keep sprigs of rosemary nearby, to protect them from evil. But I knew better. I was defended with my nails and my thorns. I wore boots with nails, a scarf of black thorns.

One time when I was leaving town with my heavy backpack, a woman I recognized, a teacher of mine, called out for me to be careful on the road. She was kindhearted, and I remembered her lessons in language and history. But she wasn't my teacher anymore. I waved, but I hadn't learned anything new from her. I already knew that danger was everywhere.

I took a different route home each time to ensure that no one would follow Onion and me. I favored paths so rocky and steep, anyone else would have stumbled. It was the season when the earth turned red and yellow, when the whole countryside was blessed with orange light, but not anymore. Usually the leaves changed slowly: rubies, garnets, amber. This year, they had all dropped off at the same time.

This was the season when my sister and I had gathered fallen apples from the trees in our neighbor's orchard. The old woman would chase us away, shouting and throwing stones that dropped harmlessly on the grass. Now, the orchards were bare and the apple trees were as fruitless as fence posts. The hillsides were black; the road littered with garbage. Feral house cats living in the ditches would claw at any kindness, and Onion was so afraid of these wild cats, I had to carry him when they hissed and showed their claws.

I tried to avoid the looters who had wrecked my garden. I'd heard they'd taken up residence near the river, at a place made out of half-dead timbers they called the forgetting shack. Some slept beneath bridges, but they all gathered at the fire they kept burning when the dark began to fall. I could smell smoke coming from their direction. When I held up my hands to the east, where they were gathered, I could feel their pain, a kind of pain that was much worse than what I did to myself with my ink and my pins.

Once in a while, the looters arrived at a house in town in the middle of the night, threatening the citizens, demanding food. Most of them were no older than me, a few were only eleven or twelve. They had lost their parents, and, one by one, they'd run away from their empty homes. They drank gin until they were dizzy. They made themselves sick with whatever they found in their parents' medicine cabinets, tablets to make them woozy with dreams, pills that kept them up all night.

I had seen Heather Jones, the girl I knew who had joined them, panhandling on a corner. She had woven a hundred braids in her hair, and she wore what had once been a beautiful white dress. People walked by without looking, they didn't want to see the emptiness in her eyes, but I put some coins in her tin. I didn't wait for her to thank me. That's not why I did it. It was because I remembered the white dress she wore, how pretty she'd looked in school, how jealous I'd been. Now, the fabric was torn from the brambles she slept upon. Now, it was closer to gray.

I could hear the looters every once in a while, music rising from down at the forgetting shack at the river. I felt protected by my bad reputation and the nails I hammered into the trees all around my house, a warning not to come near. But sometimes I'd wake in the night and I'd listen to their music. I couldn't help myself. Voices carried on the wind, and their voices called to me. Several times, I'd left my sister in my dreams, and risen from my bed under the table. The loneliness I felt cut right through me, and not even sleep could ease my sorrow on nights such as these.

Help me, my sister called in my dreams, but I no longer went to her to help her carry water from the well, or sweep the floor, or close the window.

One night I went out very late. I made my way through the woods to see the forgetting shack for myself. I watched the looters dancing until their feet were bruised. Their bodies were covered with sweat. Some of them howled, and the sound went down my spine. Some of them spun in circles, until they looked like spires of silver.

Standing there alone, I swayed in time with the music. There were drums and tambourines. There was the organ they'd stolen from the church and the flutes they'd taken from the school music room. But this music was different from anything I'd heard before. It was something that scared me and made me want to be closer to it at the very same time.

I thought dancing with the looters would be like jumping into the fire. I would never have to think again. All I had to do was join them, do as they said, follow their lead, forget everything that had come before.

I laughed out loud at the notion and my laughter made them turn to me, all at once. The boys I'd gone to school with were all looking at me. Most of them had never noticed me before. Now I could probably have any one of them, if that's what I'd wanted. They were lonely the way I was. I could dance all night long with any boy I chose. I could forget right along with them.

They started to call to me as if they knew me. They started to come nearer. They thought I was Green, too shy to speak. Green, who had patience and pretty long hair. Green, who would dance with anyone who asked, anyone who grabbed her, anyone who pulled her closer to the fire.

Leave her alone, a girl shouted. It was Heather Jones in her dirty white dress. She was drunk, but she recognized me. *Does she look like she's one of us?*

Now the boys examined me closely. They saw the black roses and ravens on my skin. They noticed the nails on my boots, and my clothes, covered with thorns, so that anyone who tried to touch me would surely bleed.

They ran from me then, as though I were the dangerous one. They went back to their fire as if they'd never even noticed me standing so close by. I went home, grateful to Heather for calling out. She knew I wasn't like them. All the same, I understood what they were after. I understood wanting to forget. Things that made you remember cut like pieces of glass. A song, a memory, a blade of grass, a white dress, a dream, all of it as painful as the deepest wound.

I went home and locked my door. I was glad to be away from those pathetic creatures at the forgetting shack who didn't know how to face the darkness of their lives. That wasn't me. Heather Jones was right. I wasn't afraid of the dark. I didn't mind a certain kind of pain. I welcomed it because it took me away from my loss. It was better than anything at the forgetting shack. It was under my control.

I took the pins and the bottle of ink and held them close. Every night I tattooed more black thorns, vines, roses, bats. When I had less skin to cover, the task grew more difficult. I turned to my fingers and toes. My instep. My thigh. I had to squint and take my time. I worked hard, far into the night. Once I fell asleep still clutching my pins, spilled ink spreading across the table in a dark and endless pool.

Now when I dreamed, my sister took my hand in hers. She was still like moonlight, but fainter, more sorrowful. She whispered something I couldn't understand. It was as if we spoke different languages, as if I were losing her even in my dreams. The thorns on my skin were sharp and fierce, like me. The thorns could pierce through any dream. I grew restless in my sleep. I took to avoiding it whenever I could.

Green, my sister called to me whenever I grew so tired, I couldn't help but drift off.

It was the only word she spoke that I understood, but I couldn't answer to that name. Instead of tears there was soot in my eyes, so I called myself Ash. This was who I had become, but it was also the reason my sister stopped coming to me in my dreams after that. She didn't know me by name anymore, so how could she call to me?

When I closed my eyes to search for her, I was a stranger.

Treasure

This is who I loved

I was gathering chestnuts deep in the woods where no one ever ventured, not even the crows, when I heard something nearby. Beside me, Onion began to growl, low in his throat, the way he used to whenever hawks came too close to our garden. Whenever there were strangers in the yard.

I bent to the ground, and I could feel footsteps.

At first I thought it might be the looters, come after me.

But when I touched the air, I could feel regret in the wind.

I thought it might be the girl, Heather Jones, with her neat braids and her ruined dress. Every once in a while she left her tin outside my gate. I filled it with bread or cooked rice or a bit of sugar. Sometimes I added a small pot of my asparagus soup.

But when I pushed away the overhanging branch of an oak tree in order to peer through, I could feel hope in the stems of the singed leaves.

The few birds that were left in the woods were chattering, flapping their wings, hopping from branch to branch. I could hardly see through the shadows, but when I narrowed my eyes I observed something white moving through the bare trees. It wasn't Heather in her torn dress. She slept most of the day, along with the others from the forgetting shack, exhausted from their wild nights.

I thought it might be a ghost that approached me. My sister, perhaps, with her snow-white hair, or my mother, in her favorite white shawl, or my father, his beard gone white with the shock of what had happened to our beautiful green world.

I dropped to my knees, not caring about sticks and stones. I could feel the thorns I had sewn onto my jacket and leggings stabbing through me. I wanted my family more than I ever thought I could want anything. Any bit of them, any piece would suffice.

If it were only a ghost that I'd found, that would have been enough for me. I wouldn't have asked for more. If it were nothing more than mist I could neither touch nor hold, formed into the shapes of those I loved, so be it. As long as I could see my sister, my mother, my father, I would pay any price. Accept any answer.

But it was no one I loved there before me. Not in spirit or in body. It wasn't a ghost or an angel or an enemy. It wasn't mist or cloud or memory. It was only a dog, a huge white greyhound. She was standing motionless, the scattered leaves on the ground turning to powder beneath her paws.

I grabbed Onion to make sure he wouldn't charge only to be snapped up by the larger dog in one bite. I carried my sister's terrier and the basket of chestnuts through the woods. I had traded away nearly everything that was worth trading, but I still had to eat. I had to quiet my churning stomach. Later, I would pound the chestnuts into flour and bake bread, but if I needed to defend myself against this strange dog on the way home, the chestnuts would work as well as stones when put to use with my slingshot.

Onion growled all the way home, so I knew the other dog was following. But I couldn't see her. I didn't hear a thing. She was a stray, like so many others, but something more as well. She was a ghostdog, mist through the woods, a pale cloud, silent and graceful. When I went inside the house, I could still feel her out in the yard. I put my hand on the cool glass of the windowpane, and there she was.

She felt exactly like sorrow.

That night I baked, and while the loaves of chestnut bread cooled on the rack, I went out to the porch. I alone sat on the steps where I used to sit with my sister, back when we thought the world was ours. If Aurora walked through the gate now, she wouldn't recognize me. She'd run from the ink on my skin; she'd shy from my choppy hair and the thorns that covered me, head to toe, front to back.

It seemed so long ago that we used to sit side by side, shoulders touching as we shelled peas for supper. Whenever we husked corn, we would toss the corn silk on each other's heads and laugh until we were dizzy. We were so certain of our futures back then. We were so sure of how we would fill up those blank, white pages. We would grow old together, marry brothers, live in houses so near to each other, we would be able to hear one another singing lullabies to the children we would surely have someday.

A few stars came out and shone, glittering and far away. The ashes had all fallen to the ground and I could see the moon, silver in the sky. Like a patch of moonlight, just as white, there was the dog in the garden. I waited, because I knew it would take time before she approached. I didn't blame her for keeping her distance.

After a while, my legs began to cramp up. I wanted to go inside and bolt the door. I wanted to sleep and close my burning eyes. But I stayed where I was, on the porch, in the moonlight. I dredged up whatever patience I'd once had, back when I was Green.

At last the white dog came closer. I didn't say anything. I was afraid I might scare her away. I knew what it felt like to be alone. I knew what it was not to trust anyone. All the same, I reached out my hand, the only part of me that wasn't covered with thorns. Now that the dog was beside me, I noticed that her paws were singed, the skin patchy and oozing and black. Greyhounds were meant to run, but every step must have brought this one agony.

When the greyhound rested her muzzle in my

outstretched hand, I understood why I'd thought she was sorrow. I would have never guessed that a dog could cry, but this one did. Maybe she'd been burned by embers, like the ones in my eyes, or maybe she'd lost everyone she'd ever cared about, the way I had.

I called her Ghost. When I said her name aloud she looked up at me, and when I went inside she followed the way ghosts do, silent, but there all the same. She curled up on the stone hearth, which was cool on her burned paws. Then she slept as though she hadn't had any rest for days, her feet racing through her dreams.

My own dreams were empty that night, devoid of moonlight. Even when I closed my eyes, my sister was always just out of reach. I started in my sleep and sat up, hitting my head. I was still sleeping in the pile of quilts under the dining room table. I'd been avoiding the room I'd shared with my sister; now I dragged along the pillows and quilt and went to open the bedroom door. There was moonlight streaming through the window, and before I knew it I'd fallen asleep in my sister's bed.

In the morning, it was as if Ghost had always been there. She ate from the same bowl as Onion, and the terrier didn't seem to mind. I found a salve in my mother's medicine cabinet, made from Saint-John's-wort and yarrow. I understood that a greyhound was not a greyhound unless it could run. I called the white dog to me, and she let me apply the ointment and wrap bandages around her paws.

That next night, Ghost slept at the foot of my sister's bed. I woke only once. I thought I had felt the dog running in her sleep. I thought I heard the sound of weeping, but when I stroked the greyhound's face, there were no tears.

The next time we went into the woods, I brought along a loaf of bread and a thermos of cold, clear well-water. I had planned to go back to where the old trees grew, to gather the last of the chestnuts, but Ghost had other ideas. She wouldn't follow. She led. Her paws were still so tender, she couldn't manage any more than a trot; still, I had to run to keep up with her. In no time my heart was pounding in my chest. How fast she must be when she ran at full speed. How much she must miss racing like mist. How sad that she was forced to plod through the woods with me as I stumbled through the brambles with my eyes that only saw half of what was there, with my nail-studded boots that slowed me down.

Before I realized where we were headed, we had arrived at my neighbor's house. The house was dark, and the front gate moved back and forth in the breeze. The yard was littered with debris, broken branches, black apples, clods of mud. Nothing grew in this place but nettles, tall and bitter, stinging to the touch.

This was the house that belonged to the neighbor who had thrown stones when Aurora took apples from her orchard. We had hooted and stuck out our tongues and made faces at her. We had run across her meadow laughing, but late at night we had wondered if she was a witch who might put a spell on us for eating the golden delicious apples we had gathered.

Now that I was beside my neighbor's door, I noticed a pile of the same white stones I had found in my yard, the ones that had been carefully aimed to chase away the looters, the ones that looked like moonstones. I hadn't given a moment's thought to this old woman, but she had obviously remembered me. I knocked on the door, and when no one answered, I pushed it open. I went into the house and there she was in her kitchen with nothing to eat but birdseed. Soot covered everything. The clocks no longer told time.

Have you come to return my stones? my neighbor asked.

I have something better to give you in return, I told her.

I left the bread and the thermos of water on the table, then I took the broom, the mop, the bucket, and began to clean. I was good at it by now. With one touch, I could tell what needed care. The books on the shelf were thick with dust. The floors were coated with muck. The paintings on the wall appeared black, until they were wiped clean to reveal women whose faces resembled my neighbor, younger, prettier relatives who looked down upon me kindly for rescuing them from the ashes.

When I had finished my work, everything in my neighbor's house gleamed. I had repaid my debt to her. Now I was the only thing covered in ashes. Ashes stuck to my skin, my choppy hair, the thorns on my clothes, my black tattoos.

Green, the old woman said to me. She had eaten every crumb of the bread I'd baked and drank every drop of water from my well. I wouldn't have guessed she knew me well enough to know my name, but it was too late to call me that now.

That's who I used to be, I told her. *Now my name is Ash.*

Whatever your name is, I have a gift for you in return. It's out on my porch.

There was only a big bag of birdseed, but I carried it with me. Once I'd reached home, I left the birdseed in the garden. I guessed it was worthless. I assumed it was all the old woman had.

My hands hurt from cleaning my neighbor's house. My feet ached in my father's old boots. My skin hurt from the sharpness of the pins. I had no time for worthless gifts.

Onion followed me into the house, but Ghost would not come inside for her dinner. I fell asleep in my sister's bed, exhausted. I woke once, and when I looked in the garden I saw the greyhound, white as the moon. She was tossing the bag of birdseed into the air as though it were a toy, shaking it with her teeth.

In the morning, there were a hundred birds in the garden. I sat on the porch where I used to sit with Aurora and listened as they sang a hundred different songs. The birds had converged from everywhere, from the deepest woods, from the charred canyons of the city. There were cardinals as red as cherries, jays as blue as the sky used to be, crows with night-black feathers, swallows with graceful wings, flocks of sparrows, mourning doves the color of tears.

When the hundred birds were finished eating,

the garden was littered with the husks of pumpkin and barley seeds. Something else had been left behind as well. Two baby sparrows, dusty and ash-covered, their wings too singed to fly. I took off my jacket and shook out the thorns, then carried the sparrows nestled in the jacket's lining. I brought them into the warm kitchen.

That night I dug until I found some juicy worms.

Is it all right to eat those? I heard someone say.

It was Heather Jones in her white dress, so skinny she looked like a ghost herself. She reeked of gin, and looked woozy. Her legs were covered with sores and little burns. Still, she smiled at me as though we had once been friends. I realized that Heather was prepared to eat worms. That's how famished she was.

I brought out some tins of beans, a loaf of bread, a few asparagus. I wished I'd had more. I'd been trying and failing to fish down at the river, and I couldn't think of anything else I could spare.

Then I remembered something I'd stored away.

I ran and found a dress that had belonged to my mother, soft blue denim that wouldn't be so easily torn by the brambles in the woods. Heather held the dress up to her carefully, as if it were made out of sapphires.

Oh, she said. *How beautiful.*

I thought about how jealous I'd been of her. She'd been one of the prettiest girls in school. By now we could hear music from the forgetting shack. We could smell the billows of smoke.

I'm late, Heather said.

You don't have to go if you don't want to.

It was as polite as I had ever been, and this was as good an invitation as I could manage, but Heather just laughed. She was unsteady on her feet. When you looked closely, you could see that her features were fine. So close to her, I could smell liquor and dirt.

Don't you hear? Heather insisted when I let her know she could stay. *They're waiting for me.*

Heather ran off with the blue dress, and there was nothing I could do about it. She thought they were waiting for her. She thought she could dance her sorrow away. She must have believed she could forget that her mother and father had also gone into the city that day.

I went inside to mash the worms into a paste. My hands were even uglier now from digging, from cleaning the old woman's floors, from chopping wood. I hardly recognized them as my own. I wondered if I was only a black cloud, a spray of mist, a stone, and nothing more. I studied the black roses ringed with thorns that I had inked onto my skin. I was Ash, and these were my hands.

But when I fed the worm paste to the baby sparrows they didn't care if my hands were ugly, that my burning eyes could hardly see, that my long, black hair was hacked off, lying in a pile in a corner. When I patted the dogs, they didn't care if my boots were old, if there was dirt under my nails, if there were thorns in my clothes, sharp as knives. When I swept my neighbor's floor, she had not cared that I was covered with ashes.

Every day I baked two loaves of bread, one to share with the dogs and the sparrows, one for my neighbor on the other side of the hill. My days were divided into tasks. I collected chestnuts in the morning, baked at noon, and late in the day I visited the piles of remembrance stones in the woods, white and black and silver. In the evenings, I took out my pins. I was covered now, my feet were covered with thorns, my legs with black vines, my arms with dozens of black roses. There were two ravens on my shoulders, and after propping up a mirror, I'd managed a bat at the nape of my neck. Every now and then I found room for a black leaf or an inky bud about to bloom.

As I worked, the sparrows nested in the pile of hair in the corner. A sparrow wasn't a sparrow unless it could rise into the sky, even I knew that. Soon enough the fledglings' singed feathers had fallen out, but I didn't guess how strong their wings had become until they began to flit around the house. I didn't know what they had been busy weaving in their nest until they presented me with their gift — a fishing net made from the strands of my own black hair.

I went down to the river that very night, as far away from the forgetting shack as I could. The moon was full. Streams of silver light reminded me of my sister. She would often dance while the rest of us worked in the garden. I used to tease her for being lazy. I used to call her names and tell her she'd never amount to anything if she didn't pay attention and work harder. Now I understood that she was working hard at dancing, at laughing, at being moonlight. She wasn't like poor Heather, forgetting with every step she took. My sister was learning the world as she danced. She was understanding the earth, the air, the fire of her own blood, the falling rain that made her laugh and dance even more wildly.

My vision was so bad, it didn't matter if I went fishing in the day or the night. In fact, my weak eyes preferred the moonlight. Night was better, colder, lonelier. But I was hardly alone. The dogs had followed me and the sparrows had fluttered behind, enjoying their first flight beyond the confines of the house.

Perhaps the fish would be more likely to drift into my net while they slept. I dipped my fingers into the cool water. I could feel the currents and the dreams of the fish, fluid and silver, like my own dreams had once been. I had tried to go fishing several times and had always failed at the task. But this time was different. It was the net that must have called the fish, dark and floating in the water, a broken part of me.

I caught three fish and placed them in a bucket of river water. I wrung out the black net and folded it into my pocket. The dogs followed me, the sparrows flew above me, the shining fish swam in the bucket I carried home. I cooked one fish for the dogs and the sparrows and me, another for my neighbor, and the third I kept in the bucket on my porch, where it swam in river water like a fallen star.

That night I dreamed of Aurora, but she didn't recognize me.

Where is my sister? she called out. *What have you done with her?*

Aurora still didn't know me by my new name. She backed away from the thorns and the nails and the black roses. I tried to run to her, but the vines around my legs pulled me down. I tried to reach out to her, but the thorns on my skin pinned me to the wall.

I heard someone crying, and when I awoke the cry was in my own mouth.

I went to the window to see if there were any stars. Out on the porch, something was studying the bucket where the last fish swam. It was a hawk that perched on the rim of the bucket, ash-covered, starving. The hawk hadn't been able to hunt because his beak had been burned. I wondered how long it had been since he'd eaten. We had always chased hawks from our gardens; we called them thieves and didn't like the way they scooped up the quiet rabbits and preyed upon the field mice who burrowed near the fences.

Now, I didn't drive the hawk away. I let him

make a dinner of the third fish, down to the eyes and the bones. I wished the hawk well, certain he'd soon be on his way.

But in the morning, the hawk was still on the porch, cleaning his feathers. I dressed and went outside. Without my leather jacket, I might have been afraid of his sharp talons, but I reached out my arm and the hawk hopped on. I treated his beak with lavender oil, which my mother always said could heal nearly any burn. I knew, after all, that a hawk is not a hawk unless he can hunt.

But for now he seemed happy to perch on my shoulder. So close to me, he felt like the wind, like the highest reaches of the sky. When we went into the woods to where the old trees grew, the hawk shook so many chestnuts from the trees, I could hardly carry them all home.

That day I had enough to bake six loaves of bread. One for me and the sparrows, one for the dogs, one for my neighbor, one for the hawk, one for Heather Jones, who had taken to sleeping under the old bridge where the weeds were as tall as trees.

I realized that there was one extra loaf of bread. I wondered why I had baked the sixth loaf, not knowing the reason until I heard footsteps out in my yard. They were quiet steps, not the looters, but the steps of someone who traveled alone.

I put on my leather jacket, my nail-rimmed boots, my thorn-edged leggings, then went to open the door. He was so very still I might have easily slammed the door shut without ever knowing he was there. I might have thought it was only the night outside, only the stars and the moon. But I could feel him out there, even though he was dressed all in black, his hood drawn low so he could hide in the ashes and no one could see his face. Just a profile. Just quiet.

Some other girl might have slammed the door and put the bolt on. She might have shouted for the stranger to go away or set the dogs on him. But I wasn't just any girl. I was the one with a talent for gauging truth from dishonesty, copper from gold, green tea from black, a friend from an enemy.

Though I could barely see his face, I knew this boy was a diamond. I could tell who he was when I touched his arm. I could tell from his boots coated with mud, from his black-hooded coat. I understood how alone he was and how tired he was of running. He seemed unable to speak, but the first thing he showed me was a small portrait of his mother that he'd painted. He carried the painting close to his heart.

The boy motioned that he'd been in the city, that he and his mother had been separated when the fire began. He had already crossed the river and walked a hundred miles to look for her. Now he was too exhausted to go on. His backpack was empty except for a box of paints and a sheaf of white paper, burned at the edges.

Another girl might have been afraid of a boy who arrived with so little, who refused to show his face, who could not speak a word. But I had my armor, I had my thorns, I'd already lost everyone

I'd ever loved. I offered the boy the sixth loaf of bread. I felt I had baked it for him even before he had walked into the yard. I could tell he was starving from the way he ate, huddled against the wind, his back to me. He wasn't about to let down his guard. He smelled like smoke and city streets.

I wasn't sure whether this boy had lost the ability to speak or whether he had simply chosen silence. Perhaps he spoke another language entirely. One I couldn't be expected to understand. That was fine with me. In silence there was truth.

I could tell who my guest was without one syllable. A boy who ran from the fire. A boy in search of his mother. When Ghost curled up at the boy's feet, when Onion didn't growl, when the sparrows ate crumbs from his hands, when the hawk perched on his shoulder, I knew I could let him stay.

I told him he could sleep in the barn. I brought out blankets and pillows. He could drink the water from the well. He could eat from the tins of food I had traded for in exchange for silver and gold and share the soup made from asparagus.

He could look at the stars with me whenever he liked.

When I told him my name was Ash, he nodded as though the word was a gift. Because he couldn't tell me his name in return, I called him Diamond. He seemed to like that name as well. Something inside him shone through the dark even though he kept his face hidden, hood pulled down. When he'd gone off across the yard to sleep, I thought perhaps I dreamed him up. A hallucination made out of loneliness, black ink, sorrow. Perhaps he'd never existed in the first place. But even when he'd gone and was already sleeping, I could see something bright everywhere he'd walked. It was almost like having moonlight again.

Rain

This is what I lost

Diamond didn't speak and I could hardly see; maybe that was why we got along so well. I, who preferred stones to flesh and blood, who kept away from people, could not spend enough time with Diamond. I knew him in a way I couldn't explain, the way I knew silver from gold, the way I knew the weather. When we listened to the wind together, we understood exactly what it was saying. When we sat close in the dark, we could feel each other's broken hearts beating.

Together, we stopped being hungry. We ate the bread I baked. Diamond fixed a soup out of beans and rice, simple but filling and tasty. Once, I asked him if his mother had taught him the recipe. Although he didn't speak, I could tell that the answer was yes. He took out the little painting of her, so carefully rendered in watercolors, and he didn't need to say more.

I knew he was thinking of her every time I heard him hum a certain tune, a lullaby she'd surely taught him. I hoped for his sake that his mother had managed to find safety when the fire began.

There was only one thing we didn't agree on. Diamond believed that the garden would grow. The topsoil was ashy and gray, and I told him not to bother with it, but Diamond wouldn't listen. All winter long, he carted the bad soil away. He spent hours picking out stones, which I brought to the piles in the darkest woods. Black for my mother, silver for my father, white as snow for my sister, a pile of moonstones.

You shouldn't even try, I told him each time he set to work. *Nothing will ever grow here.*

I showed him the looters' tracks, the broken fences, the pumpkin seeds left by the birds, the rock-hard earth. He just kept at it. I could hear him raking at night, as if he could work away his grief. For some reason I slept easier when I heard him. The sound of his working became as familiar as the wind, as rainfall, as the beat of a heart.

I still looked for Heather Jones. I worried that she would disappear, but it was easy enough to find her. During the daylight hours she was usually asleep under the bridge, her skin mottled from too much gin, the braids in her hair undone, her clothes dank from rainwater. I left pots of Diamond's stew for her, along with bottles of clean well-water. I knew Heather had been drinking from the ashy shallows of the river. She'd been eating mud just to fill her stomach.

Heather laughed sometimes when she recognized me, but it was the kind of laughter that sounded like a cry.

I could tell that she'd danced too close to the fire at the forgetting shack because she'd singed the hem of my mother's blue dress. She didn't seem to notice, and I didn't mention it. She was in a haze, trapped in the foggy ground between forgetting and living.

Still, we understood each other. If the world had been a different place, we might have been friends.

One day, Heather stared at me and grinned. She almost looked pretty. *Something's changed*, she declared. *You don't look the same.*

It was still me, my black tattoos, my leather jacket, my thorns, but Heather was right. I could feel a change inside, one I didn't yet comprehend.

When I went to my neighbor's to take her fresh water and fish I had caught with my net, I asked if she thought I seemed the same, the girl with ink on her skin.

The old woman didn't say a word. Instead, she led me to the staircase, where there were the ashy portraits I'd cleaned. Now my neighbor told me to try to guess which one she was. I studied the portraits carefully, but I had no idea which she might be. They looked familiar, but one girl was too pretty, one was too sad, one was too silly to be my neighbor.

Guess, my neighbor insisted. *Go on. Which one do you think I am?*

Still, I could not tell.

Look closely, she said, but even when I did, I had no idea.

At last I gave up. *Who are you?* I asked.

Each and every one, my neighbor told me. She shook her head as though I were a child rather than a girl about to turn sixteen. *Did you think nothing ever changed?*

Was it Diamond's arrival that had made the difference? Did it make it easier to listen to the wind with someone beside me? Wasn't the wind just as cold and harsh? Why would I feel any less abandoned? Wasn't I still alone in my thoughts? I already had the company of Onion and Ghost and the sparrows and the hawk and my neighbor on the other side of the hill. What did I need with this boy, who ate more than his fair share and filled the air with clouds of dust as he worked in the garden?

It was a puzzle I couldn't solve. After a while I stopped trying. Diamond was there, like the white dog and the sparrows and the hawk. A guest in my house, nothing more. He was there, like the wind and the stars up above.

I didn't understand for the longest time why I let Diamond stay. I watched him painting with the few watercolors he had left, and I felt as if something inside me was part of that paint, that white, singed paper, that paintbrush.

I didn't understand until one day when I went into the woods to search for chestnuts. That was when I realized I was singing. My voice sounded thin and unfamiliar to my own ears.

The next afternoon, I was wringing out the

wash to hang on the line when I realized I was dancing. My feet seemed too graceful to belong to me, even in my father's old boots.

The following evening, while I was polishing the last of the silver to trade, I happened to gaze into the platter my mother always used on holidays. Even I could see there was a smile on my face.

Something had indeed happened to me. This was not the way I ordinarily behaved. I was not someone who danced and sang and smiled at her own reflection. I was Ash, the girl with thorns on her clothes, the one who preferred stones to people.

When I next went to my neighbor's house I took along a pot of the stew Diamond had made. The old woman uncovered the pot and breathed in the scent of beans and rice. Then she told me to sit down.

She ladled out a bowlful for herself and one for me.

Did the boy cook this? she asked after she took one bite.

When I nodded, she looked at me closely, considering my face. The old woman had boiled a cup of tea for me, brewed from the stinging nettles that grew outside her door. I would have guessed the tea would be too bitter to drink, but the taste was perfect. It quenched my thirst completely.

You say your name is Ash, the old woman said thoughtfully.

I say it because it's true, I told her.

I had a tickle in the back of my throat. The feeling that some people get when they tell a lie. Quickly, I drank more nettle tea.

Is it?

My neighbor laughed then, as if she knew something I didn't know. She had already told me that everything changes. Now she wanted me to know more. She brought out a magnifying glass. When I peered through the glass I could see that one of the black vines tattooed around my ankle had turned green. It was the green of apple trees when they were first in leaf.

In my mouth, there was the taste of apples, sweet and sharp.

What do you think has happened? the old woman asked me. *Think hard.*

It's a trick of the ink, I told her. *Nothing more.*

All the same, I walked home slowly. I tried to figure out the puzzle I had become. I carefully tied the scarf of thorns around my neck. I kicked at the dust with my heavy, nail-studded boots. I didn't sing or dance or smile. I spat on the ground. I was Ash, after all.

But the taste of apples stayed with me.

In the evenings, after supper, Diamond sat at the table and painted. He hummed while he worked, and the sound made me think of what I had lost. I wished my sister could have danced to the song Diamond's mother had taught him. I wished when I closed my eyes, she was still with me.

I had no idea that Diamond was working on a portrait of me until he gave me the painting. At first I didn't know who it was. The girl I saw didn't look like me. There were no thorns, no nails, no bats, no vines, no black roses.

I'm not this pretty, I said. *My sister was the one who looked like moonlight.*

Diamond shook his head. He motioned for me to come close, and when I did, he touched my forehead.

I still couldn't see his face beneath the black hood. I couldn't see the look in his eyes. But I understood. I knew that he'd painted not only what he'd seen, but what he'd felt deep inside.

The next time I went to my neighbor's house I brought another pot of stew. On this day, the old woman had made bread out of nettles. Although this loaf was not half as sweet as the bread I baked, I ate every bit.

Do you still say your name is Ash? my neighbor asked when I had finished eating, when I had washed the plates and set them to dry, when I had swept the floor and straightened the portraits on the staircase.

It's still true, I told her.

She gave me the magnifying glass and told me to look at my hands. When I did I saw that the leaves that had been black were now green. It was the green of newly cut grass. In my nose, there was the scent of summer, fresh enough to make me sneeze.

I blew my nose on my handkerchief, but I could still smell cut grass.

It's the ink, I said. *Not me.*

I didn't believe the garden would grow, but I must have believed in Diamond. The next time I went into town I brought along my mother's pearl necklace to trade for packets of seeds. I had found the necklace in a drawer, set in a velvet box, tied up with ribbons. Beside the box was a card made out to me. My mother had planned to give me her pearls on my sixteenth birthday. Now I wasn't sure that day would come. The last thing I wanted was pearls. I thought my mother would understand and agree with me. I thought she would want me to choose lettuce and scallions and herbs above pearls.

I traded for the seeds and for something else — a denim jacket for Diamond. I thought it might suit him when he wanted to toss away that black coat with the hood that smelled like smoke. When he was ready to show me his face.

While I was getting ready to go I heard the shopkeeper and his wife talk about the people who had destroyed the city. Some of them had been living among us, pretending to be good neighbors. Their wives had shopped in our markets. Their children had gone to our schools, eaten our bread, played in our streets.

Many of their children had burned right along with others. Still others were wanderers, their families devastated. In the storekeeper's opinion it was easy enough to tell who these wanderers were. They would not look at you directly. Often they were burned. Even more often, they refused to speak.

I felt as though I had swallowed stones. Was it possible that my talent had failed me? That I had not been able to distinguish a friend from an enemy?

I walked through the woods without thinking of where I was going. I wanted to be lost, but I knew these woods too well. I could hear the music from the forgetting shack. I could hear laughter rising over the hill. I thought about the path that would lead me there. It was easy enough to find. I started down to the shack, slowed by my nail-studded boots. Halfway down the overgrown path I stopped. I had spied Heather.

She was curled up beside the fire, so close that sparks fell into her hair. People did their best to pull her away, but she crawled right back. She was long past listening to anyone. She was barely Heather Jones anymore. She was disappearing a little more each day, so thin, so frail, a wisp of smoke. One day she would surely vanish altogether, and there was no way to stop her. She was so busy forgetting, she couldn't take a single step into the future.

I turned and went through the woods. I wasn't interested in tablets or gin or sleeping pills or burning up alive. I had something far better to erase any facts that were too painful to remember. I could hear the hundred birds nesting in the treetops. I could hear the wind whispering that it would soon rain.

As soon as I got home I took out my blackest ink. I lit a candle, then sorted my needles and pins from the most delicate to the sharpest. I had one pin that was like a strand of silver, another that was like a sigh, a third that was as cold as a chip of ice, and a dozen more so tiny, I had to feel for them because they were all but invisible. Pain wasn't the thing I feared most.

I could hear the dogs running in their sleep. I could hear the sparrows fluttering their wings. Dreaming of the hunt, the hawk stretched out his great yellow talons. Diamond must have been asleep in the barn after a day of working in the hopeless garden. That was just as well. I didn't want to see him. I didn't want his silence, his black hood. I didn't want him as a friend or an enemy.

I could still see the bit of green on my ankle. That vine. That leaf. That rose. The color was a mistake. I wanted to announce who I was, not change back. I was Ash, who wanted black and stones, leather and thorns. I took my mother's mirror and rested it on a pile of my father's books. Now I could see my own handiwork, even with my blurry vision and the darkness of the night.

I had one place left, a circle above my heart.

I used the needle that felt like ice. It was the sharpest of all.

I was making a different sort of heart, one that was black, one that was protected by thorns, by bats, by raven's wings, by sorrow, by my aloneness, my armor.

I was halfway through this last tattoo when Diamond walked through the door. He was so silent, I could barely hear him. He was so quiet, I didn't know he was there until he took my hand in his. He raised the pin up to the place where his own heart was. He made it clear what he wanted me to do.

I gave him the other half of my heart. I worked until my fingers were numb, until our loss mirrored each other's. I used the ice needle, the one that caused the greatest pain.

I watched to see if Diamond flinched, but he never once did. I etched half a rose, half a wing, half a thorn, half a leaf. When I was done, Diamond took off his black hood so I could see what the fire had done to him. Then I understood why pain meant nothing to him anymore. I could see why half was enough for him. One side of his face was perfect, my Diamond. The other half was charred and discolored. I kissed both sides. They were one and the same to me.

I could feel the season changing. It was growing warmer every day. I felt it as though I were a leaf that was greening, a vine that was growing toward the sun.

One day the sparrows rose high in the sky, then

settled in the treetops. I forced myself not to call them back to me. I knew they were meant to fly.

Soon after the hawk disappeared from my porch. I would see him sometimes, his wingspan nearly blocking out the sun. He peered down from above, but I didn't whistle for him. I didn't wave so that he would light on my arm. I didn't insist that he eat grain from my hand. I knew that hawks had to hunt.

All the same, I considered putting a collar and a leash on Ghost. I knew she was next. I could tell by the way she stared into the woods. One morning when the air was especially fresh and Diamond was watering the garden, I left Onion inside the new fence Diamond had built. I felt the leaves, the vines, the warming air. I went out walking with Ghost.

We went past the oldest trees, past the piles of stones, to the deepest part of the woods. Even I who knew these woods so well could have lost my way here, but the white dog knew where to go. We both knew what she needed to do.

In the treetops there were the hundred birds who had come to eat birdseed from my garden. There were the sparrows who had knitted a fishing net from my own black hair. There was the hawk whose wingspan could block out the sun.

I knelt down beside the white dog. I could feel her trembling. That's how badly she wanted to run.

She had slept on my sister's bed with me. She had dreamed right alongside me. She had led me to places I never would have gone if I hadn't followed her. She looked up at me, and I called her Ghost one last time. Then I let her go.

Not long after that, Heather Jones disappeared. She was not at the place where she usually slept, beneath the bridge. When I left out food and clothes for her, no one collected the packages. When I looked for her footsteps in the mud, they weren't there.

I went down to the forgetting shack to search for her. It was early morning, and most of the people there were still asleep. Their feet were bloody from dancing all night. Their hair was threaded with brambles. I found two girls I might have recognized if they hadn't been so filthy and so drunk. They were settling down to sleep, but they nodded when I asked about Heather. She was gone, it was true. No one had seen her for days.

There were those who wondered what had happened to her, but they were too tired to look for her, too busy forgetting. Some people said she had drifted into the fire as she danced one dark night. She had tripped, she had fallen, she had turned into smoke. When I looked in the fire they always kept burning, there were bits of blue among the ashes.

When I left the forgetting shack, I went to visit my neighbor. My nail-studded boots hurt my feet, my leather jacket slowed me down, but at last I reached the old woman's house. I thought about Heather Jones. I thought about how it was impossible to forget, no matter how hard anyone might try.

I knocked on the door, and the old woman was waiting for me. She had made a soup out of well-water and nettles. It was thin and lukewarm, but the taste was just what I needed, bitter on my tongue.

Tell me your name, my neighbor said.

I could see the girl my neighbor had once been reflected in her eyes, in the way she held her hands, in the way she laughed at me now.

Speak up, she said. *Say it out loud.*

Ash, I insisted. *Only Ash.*

My neighbor handed me the magnifying glass, and when I looked at my arms I could see that each black rose I had inked there had turned white with a green center, the night-blooming flowers of my dreams. I could feel something green growing inside me. Green as summer in my bones. I ran all the way home. I ran through mud and brambles and thorns.

But I could feel it still.

If sparrows were meant to fly, and hawks to hunt, and greyhounds to run, then a boy such as

Diamond was meant to search for his mother. If he didn't go, if he forgot or thought of himself first, then he wouldn't be Diamond. I knew that. I wasn't surprised when I reached the gate and saw him standing there, carrying his backpack, wearing the denim jacket I'd gotten in exchange for pearls. I understood why he couldn't stay.

So I gave him a map, a thermos of clear water, a loaf of the bread I had baked. I gave him half of my heart to take with him, no matter what road he turned onto.

If he'd had a voice he would have said good-bye, he would have told me he would surely miss me the same way I'd miss him. Instead, he held me close before he set out toward the road. Instead, he kissed me and I knew these things without a single word being said.

Sister

This is the story I tell

My sister came back to me in my dreams. I could see that Aurora wasn't my age. She wasn't my twin. She was only a little girl, one I would miss every day of my life. Now that I was Green again, Aurora recognized me. She called out my name, and I was Green through and through.

I told my sister I didn't think I could live without her, but she assured me that was something I would never have to do.

I'm with you forever, she told me.

Right away, I knew it was true. True for my father, who could whistle to the birds in the trees. True for my mother, who had such gentle hands. True for my sister, who shone like silver.

When I woke from my dream I was crying. I cried like the rain, like the river that flowed to the city, and all my tears were green. At last my eyes were cleared of embers. At last I could fully see. There was daylight out my window. There were the seedlings Diamond had grown in the garden. There was the world waiting outside, aching and ruined, but beautiful all the same.

I went out and worked until I was sweating in the sun. While I worked, I missed my father and my mother. I missed the white dog and the sparrows and hawk. I missed Diamond and I missed Heather Jones.

Most of all I missed my sister.

I thought about them every day. I thought about them while I weeded between the rows, while I soaked the ground with well-water, while I raked away what was left of the ashes. Before long, the vines from the pumpkin seeds left by the sparrows were a hundred yards long. The seedlings were as high as my waist. By spring, the vines of sweet peas were taller than I was. When the warm weather returned, Onion could hide between the stalks of corn. There were hundreds of blue jays and sparrows that came to sing to me while I worked. There were white clouds drifting across the sky.

It was so hot, I took off my leather jacket. I took off my scarf made of thorns, my father's old boots. At night I dreamed of my sister, and she knew me as well as I knew myself. I dreamed of vines and grass, apples and emeralds, rain and white night-flowers that bloomed with green centers. I dreamed of everything I'd lost and all that I'd found and everything in between.

On the day I turned sixteen, I went to stand on the hillside. There were more and more lights to be seen on the other side of the river. People were moving back. The city was being rebuilt. Golden by daylight, silver at night. I could hear hammering as people from our town rebuilt the bridge. They worked all hours, they used every nail in the county, every spare set of hands.

By the end of the growing season, I'd be able to take my vegetables into the city. I'd buy myself a scale and measure out the peas and the peppers carefully, as my mother always had. I'd whistle the tunes my father had loved. I'd shop at the stores that had been both my sister's and my favorites: the bookstalls, the candy kiosks.

Wherever I went, gold dust would stick to my feet. Silver would shine in my dark hair. On every avenue, every street corner, every sidewalk, I'd carry my sister close to me, inside my heart.

Today, on the first day of being sixteen, I took three stones and went far into the woods. Without the nail-studded boots, I no longer tripped over brambles. Without the leather jacket, I did not tire. Without the scarf of thorns, I could move through the trees like mist.

When I reached the three stacks, I bowed my head. I listened to the birds, a hundred different songs of sorrow and forgiveness. That morning the first thing I'd done after waking was to go out and search until I'd found one perfect black stone, one perfect silver stone, one stone that shone white as the moon. They were the last stones I would bring here. I knew they were the last because they felt light in my pockets, light in my hands. I knew because I could remember without them.

When I left the woods to celebrate my birthday at my neighbor's house, it was twilight. All along the hillsides, everything looked green in the fading light. A few of the oak trees had managed to send out some wavering leaves. The hardiest plants, witch hazel and old ferns, were growing in the ditches. I took my time and watched the green in all its shades. I treaded gracefully, as my mother once had. I took even strides, as my father had. Onion followed me, as he used to follow my sister.

When I arrived at my neighbor's house she

went to the stove and ladled out a stew made from all the vegetables I'd brought her. It was a gift from Diamond, every bit of it. It was the garden he'd grown when I'd still refused to believe in anything. Sometimes I wondered if he hadn't watered the seedlings with his tears, and if the tears hadn't turned to silver. Everything he'd grown was filled with light.

When we'd devoured every spoonful of our dinner, my neighbor brought out a cake made of nettles. There was no icing, no candles, and the color was faintly green. A cake such as this should have been too bitter to eat, but I found I preferred it to any I'd had before. I ate every crumb, and still wanted more.

What do you call yourself now? the old woman wanted to know.

She didn't have to ask twice. For the first time since the day when it happened, I said my name out loud. The word tasted sweet as apples, fresh as grass, fragrant as roses. When I looked down I could see that the half-tattoo I shared with

Diamond had turned green around the edges. In the center, it was red.

My heart was opening.

You made it happen, my neighbor told me. *You are the ink,* she said. *Write as you want.*

It was Green who thanked the old woman, who ran home, greener with every step. Green, who was covered with bright vines, with roses that had emerald centers and only bloomed at night. Green, who threw away the ragged scarf, who cast off the leather jacket, the old boots, the ravens, the bats, the thousand thorns.

I went to the table and opened the bottle of ink, meaning to spill it all out. By chance, I took a pen and dipped it in the bottle. I saw then that the ink was green. It was the ink of a sister, a woman with long, dark hair, a man who was strong. It was the ink of a witness, of a girl of sixteen who had no idea what the future might bring. Green as the world we once knew.

I found a ream of white paper in a desk drawer. Then I understood the path my mother had spoken of for me. Every white page looked like a garden, in which anything might grow.

I sat down at the table with the pen and the ink. I spread out the clean, white pages.

Then and there, I began to tell their story.

With gratitude and love

to my dear publisher, Jean Feiwel,

and my wonderful editor, Elizabeth Szabla.

Many thanks also to Elizabeth Parisi

for her brilliant design.

To Matt Mahurin, thank you, thank you,

for pure genius.

Green Witch

Green Witch

ALICE HOFFMAN

Green Witch

Stone

Witch

This is what I remembered

What you dream, you can grow.

Someone told me that, but I didn't believe it.

    I said I had nothing and that people with nothing are unable to dream. But I was wrong. Dreams are like air. They never leave you. It takes less than nothing to begin. Start with a pile of rocks. Moonstones, night stones, stones the color of snow. Start with heartache, thorns, vines. Let there be mud on your clothes, nails in your boots, ink on your skin, pain deep inside you. Let it grow and don't be afraid.

Start with your own story.

I lost everything — my mother, my father, my sister, Aurora. They went into the city on the day of the disaster. My last words to them were not pretty. I wanted to be the one to cross the river. I was hurt and resentful. I wanted more. But I was the one who stayed home to work in the garden. It was my sister's turn to visit the city that I loved so much, not mine.

I wasn't with them when they died.

Afterward, I didn't want to move forward from that moment when our world fell apart. My garden was chalk and ashes after the city across the river burned down. Cinders covered the countryside. But time changes things, like it or not. Now, a year later, whatever I plant grows overnight. I can hear my garden in my dreams, unfolding, flourishing. Each morning I have to take an ax and cut back the vines or my cottage will disappear into the thicket.

Every one of my roses is blood red. Red to remind me of all that is gone — my family, my city, the life I led before. Blood red to remind me that despite everything, I'm alive. I'm still bleeding.

A few survivors managed to escape. They set out on rafts even though the river itself was on fire, every wave roiling with embers. Those who made it to our shores told us that the people who destroyed the city call themselves the Horde. They had been coming down from the mountains in secret for years, setting up shops, befriending their neighbors in the city, biding their time.

Once the city had been destroyed, they announced that their mission was to put an end to everything we had built. They said we had only ourselves to blame for what happened — the sheets of flame, the skies of death. They believed it wasn't their fires that had destroyed us, but what we had built — our trains and libraries and bridges, even our schools — that had brought us to ruin. They want to go back to a time when men toiled in the fields without plows and trucks, when women were shut into their houses, sweeping, cooking, never daring to speak back.

They insist the fire that killed so many was an act of heaven meant to punish us for our sins. *Repent*, they tell us. *Join with us. Don't even try to fight, because heaven is on our side. Angels ride on the backs of our black horses.*

But my sister, Aurora, was there in the city that day, selling vegetables from our truck, and I know she hadn't sinned. She was a globe of light, a white dove. Heaven would have never burned her alive.

Only a year ago, the world seemed dead. We hid in our houses. We cursed our fate. Some of us used our regret and grief to destroy ourselves. Everywhere you went, people were in shock, wondering why they had survived when so many had not.

I know. Twelve months have passed, but often it's the only thing I can see, even when I close my eyes. I was on the hillside when my family set up our vegetable stand in our favorite marketplace. I saw the spark, the flames, the red walls that trapped everyone I loved.

That day I stood on our side of the river and had no choice but to look. I looked until I couldn't see anything anymore.

I watched as my world disappeared.

Now there are buds on the trees. There are fish in the river — silver eels, trout with blue scales. The Horde keeps a watchful eye on us, but they have allowed the bridge to the city to be rebuilt, made of logs and rope and hard work. Our village has begun to trade with the few survivors who remain in the city. Some of those who were there when the explosions happened are burned. Some are mute and some are so easily startled they dart away whenever they see birds in the sky. They live underground, equally frightened by the light and the darkness. They no longer trust strangers. They appear in the marketplace when they are desperate. They offer those who come to trade with them gold and diamonds in exchange for barrels of clean water, blankets, clothes for their children. Nothing works in the city. There are no church bells, no trains, no radios, no schools, no stores. Still, whenever they're asked if they want to leave, the few who remain always refuse.

We'll rebuild, they say. *It will just take time.*

In our village, life has moved forward. We once relied on the city for nearly everything, including our clothes, our building materials, our water. Now a well stands in the center of the town square, and the water we draw in wooden buckets is clean and cold. An old man who was a professor at the university in the city has taught some local boys how to build the windmills that dot the fields. It has been difficult piecing back together all we once had. We are lucky to have the Finder, a mysterious person who lives in the woods. This curious individual leaves out parts of machines that are useful. If you need it, he can find whatever you desire among the ruins of villages that have been deserted. No one has seen the Finder, but there are many strange people in the countryside now.

The world has changed, so it only makes sense that people have changed as well. There are women who live in trees, men who sit on rooftops keeping watch for looters, bands of orphans who refused to come back to town until the woman who had been our teacher gathered them up like wildflowers. There's Uncle Tim, who is nobody's uncle but seems kindly enough and has been adopted by the village. He washed up onshore after the fires and now cares for abandoned dogs at his campsite in the woods.

These are the people who can't get past that

terrible day. We know them, and leave them to their grief. We avoid the woman who sits at the banks of the river and howls when the moon is full. We never bother the man who lost his beloved and has torn out all his hair. Loss does different things to different people. Some fall apart. Some, like the Finder, rebuild. I have done both. I have crawled under my table and refused to come out. I have covered myself with thorns and tattoos. I have planted a garden, reached out to my neighbors, begun to write down my story.

Surely, I can never sit in judgment of the lost or the found.

If you want something from the Finder, it's easy enough. Write a note and leave it in the notch of the big elm tree at the fork in the road. Leave a gift alongside. Not money — we don't use that anymore. Something useful — a set of measuring spoons or a can of soup, a hammer or an apple pie. Whatever you're looking for will be there within the week. It may be battered, it may be in pieces, but still, it will arrive. The Finder has managed to avoid the Horde's spies by limiting his movements to the cover of darkness. Because of his efforts, there are now generators that are run by hand. Lights flicker in the darkness. There are iceboxes, stoves, medicine kits. Because of him, a bell has been found to sit atop town hall. It rings twice a day, at dawn and at dusk, reminding us there are still hours in the day.

I had always been a city girl at heart. Moving there had been my dream. That was no longer true. The city I'd loved was in ruins. I thought of it as a graveyard, the past, not the future.

On the day of the bridge reopening, when a big festival was held, I couldn't go any farther than the tollgate. I stood there with my sister's little dog, Onion, beside me. I couldn't take another step.

There were jugglers on the bridge and Uncle

Tim played the guitar. The schoolteacher had the children make banners.

I walked away.

I wasn't ready to see the place where my family had perished. I couldn't go back to the city I had always loved. I have heard there are no longer bodies in the streets or blood on the cobblestones, but my beloved city is still in pieces, the buildings like silver stars — some fallen, some rising, some constant in the sky.

I live alone in my cottage, deep in the woods. I rarely go into the village. I'm too busy working in my garden. I wear simple clothes: a green shirt, a faded skirt, green suede boots or bare feet. I tie up my long black hair with string. People in the village are polite. But they stare at me because of my tattoos even though I am their neighbor and they all know my name. Green, who can be depended on. Green, who has walked through to the other side of sorrow.

Sometimes when they stare I wonder if they can see something I can't.

All through the winter, people came to me when they were hungry. They begged at my fence. Neighbors I had known in another lifetime, people who had always ignored me — the sheriff, the mayor, the shopkeeper's wife who had tried to cheat me in exchange for my mother's candlesticks and jewelry — all asked for my help. I have become someone they turn to. I can tell the false from the real, the truth from a lie, just as I am certain that when the leaves of a plum tree curl inward there are beetles at work in the bark. I know that when I reach my hands into the soil, my garden will heal and grow.

I had been Green, too shy to speak to strangers. Green, who kept her inner self hidden away. I am someone different now. They come to me not just for apples and lettuce, but for advice, remedies, solace. I try to be of help. I remember my mother's kindness, my father's strength, my sister's delight in the beauty of the world. I think of what they might have said or done.

Women stand by my fence and cry over lost love until I offer them packets of mint tea to help them sleep at night. Children beg for sweets knowing I'll give them strawberries and honey, or slices of rhubarb pie. The town councilmen ask me when the corn should be planted and where the new well should be dug.

I stand in the meadow until the sun strikes me at noon and say, *Plant here.*

I point to the place where the swamp cabbages grow, a marshy spot, the mark of an underground spring. *Here,* I tell them. *Dig your well.*

There is something else I'm known for. Another reason they come to me.

I tell their stories.

When embers whirled across the river, books were the first thing to burn. The school turned to ash. Our library has no roof. The few editions that remain are mostly unreadable. The print has dripped off the pages, pooling into inky rivers on the floorboards. Mice live in the stacks, eating the bookbinding glue, tearing up what remains of atlases and encyclopedias for their nests. Any volumes that were left were used as fuel, tossed into fireplaces and stoves during that first harsh winter.

I began by writing on myself, ink and pins on my own skin. I covered myself with tattoos, but when I was done, I still had more stories to tell. I started to write on clean white pages, the last of the paper that was left. I wrote about my family going to the city to sell vegetables, about my school friend Heather, who had lived in the woods, then disappeared, and about a boy I had never expected to walk past the garden gate, into my life. I wrote about who I was and who I would become and who I wanted to be.

When I ran out of ink, I made my own from

the sap of the black lilies that grow in the far-thest fields. It's an extract from the flower's heart; it won't wash away or smear.

Because they know I'm a writer, people in the village come to me. Even those who rarely speak, who seem closed off, who prefer to run away and hide rather than converse, arrive at my door. Some wear shawls over their heads as they come up the steps. They don't want to be seen. Each has a different story, but they all pose a single question once their stories have been told. Why did they live when so many others did not? Why have they lost all they treasured most in this world?

One after the other they sit at my kitchen table, where my mother once shelled peas, where my father drank his coffee, rich with sugar and cream, where my sister painted watercolors of our family, our garden, our life. It's here that the townspeople tell me the stories of their lives. The mistakes they made, the people they loved, the way it all used to be before the world as we knew it disappeared.

There are other people who trail after me when I come to town, desperate to talk, holding tight to my sleeve. These people have so much to say, a single volume isn't enough. They're the ones who know that our stories are all we have now.

Before long, I had written down so many stories I ran out of paper. I began to make my own. I used chopped-up rags and celery stalks, boiled oak leaves, water, ground chestnut flour. Maybe that's why some people whisper about me, even the ones who depend on me for their vegetables and fruit, who wouldn't have made it through the winter without me. They've seen the kettle I keep in the yard, set over a stack of burning wood. They've seen the plumes of black smoke rise.

When the mixture in the cauldron has turned soupy, I push it through a screen from an old window and let it dry in sheets set out in the sun until they harden. Then I cut the sheets with a pair of gardening shears.

At last, there it is.

I am the first to make paper again. If anything is magic, this is. I dream of paper as if it were a garden, sheaves of white and green, fields of it, reams of it, all smelling like spring. I never realized how beautiful paper was before. I took it for granted. I didn't rub it between my fingers or hold it up to the light.

I add different elements depending on the person whose story needs telling. Certain ingredients are right for certain stories. When someone asks how I know what to add to the mix, I ask, *How do you know the difference between the sun and the moon?* The answer is obvious, at least to me.

For the old man who knows about windmills, I added grass to the paper. You might think a man who'd once been a scientist at a university would want a clean white page, but he told me how windmills could create energy, run water pumps, turn everything green.

For the baker, who had lost his only son in the city on the terrible firestorm day, I added cloves and the last of the cinnamon from a metal container in my mother's baking cupboard. He held the paper up to his nose and breathed deeply, then wept. His story was a true baker's book — recipes for strudel and pecan pie and Sacher tortes, things we didn't have the ingredients for anymore, mythical cakes and pies that made my mouth water.

For the woman who had been my teacher, who had lost all of her books, I added a stray page I had found from her favorite novel. The paper turned a dovelike gray and smelled like heather and heath. The story my teacher dictated to me was a list of all of the novels she had loved, along with a description of exactly where she'd been when she'd read each one. She had been sprawled in a chair in the parlor of her grandmother's house right in the center of the city on a hot summer day when she'd read her favorite book of all. Because of that, and because of the incendiary nature of the love affair in the novel, the paper her story was written on was always hot to the touch.

For Uncle Tim, who was a survivor, I added ashes from that day. I had saved them in a glass bottle. When I poured in the ashes, it was like adding a storm to the mix. Uncle Tim was a hermit now because he no longer trusted men, only the stray dogs he adopted. He had seen terrible things on that day — people on fire, people leaping from ledges. He had tried to rescue several of his neighbors, but none had survived. He wept when he told his story, so I added salt. The resulting paper was black with white edges. When you ran your hand across it, tears came to your eyes.

You could hear a faraway voice say *Save me* even when no one else was in the room.

I felt it was my duty to collect these stories just as surely as if they had grown in my garden on stalks and stems, as if they had ripened in the sun and were ready to pick, one by one.

This was the way I lived now. This was the way my garden grew.

I am Green, the one to turn to, the one to whom you can tell your story. I live alone, but the villagers accept me. They need me, and because of their need, they trust me as well.

Or so I had thought.

Lately, there has been talk of witches in our midst, women they call the Enchanted. People have suspicious minds, especially in difficult times. There are those who insist my garden is the only one that flourishes because of the potions I make. They say I can mix up a remedy or a curse depending on my mood. They whisper about my tattoos. The wings of the inked bats move, people vow. The vines grow. The roses have a scent stronger than perfume.

There are those who say if I have the talents of a witch, I must be dangerous. I go out of my way to say hello to these people. I even shake their hands. Whether someone thinks I am a farmer or a sorceress makes no difference. If they believe that writing a book is casting a spell, so be it.

If this is magic, then call me a witch.

No one knows the deepest truth. How can they? I hide it well.

Even though I have never used red ink, there is half of a red heart tattooed beneath my shirt. I've been in love. That is my deepest secret. The one I'll never tell. It's no one's business but my own. His name was Diamond and he left me.

He was nearly destroyed by the fire, his face half burned, his voice lost. He was the stranger who appeared in my garden when I expected my life to be empty. He was nothing to me, and then he was everything. I helped him to heal even though I knew that meant he would go off to search for his family. I thought he would come back. I thought we were meant to be together. But I haven't even received a letter. I know letters are difficult to send in our world—still, I thought he would have managed somehow.

Being alone for so long, I've grown bitter. Every night I waited for him, and every night he disappointed me and I was more alone. On the one-year anniversary of his leaving, I made a vow that I would never let anyone near my heart again. I wouldn't even let him close.

I thought my tattoo had turned red because my heart was opening.

Now I wonder if it's nothing more than a wound that has yet to heal.

When I can't sleep, I stand at the back door and remember the way things used to be. I think about my family working in the earth and all that the earth gave back to us in return. I look out at the gathering of white doves that were once used to send messages to survivors in the city.

When the doves returned, they came back sight-less. They were considered useless after that. But I love the songs they sing. I'm honored that they visit me. When the moon is out and the trees are filled with shining white doves, more beautiful than snow, I walk outside. I climb the tree and sleep among them, listening to the wind.

I wish I could find the answer to my own question. One small bit of truth. I want to know what love is worth. If you can weigh and measure it as my mother once weighed out tomatoes and measured out green beans. I want to know if Diamond is measuring the days since we were last together, or if they mean nothing to him and I alone am counting each hour we're apart.

At night, when I hear my garden growing, I sometimes think I hear something more. I think it's the boy I love, coming back to me. I hear him say my name, even though he was made mute in the fire and I have never heard his voice. In my dreams I hear him say *I'm here with you*. He tells me not to doubt him, or myself, or what we had. But in the mornings, when I wake, I'm alone. The windows of my cottage are covered with vines. I have to pick away the roses one by one.

I have to bleed once more.

There are things in our world that are forever changed, and that is true of me as well. I am still Green, but soon I will turn seventeen, and eighteen is not far off after that. I can't go back to being the girl I once was, any more than the city I loved can rise whole from the ashes. The world is a different, sadder place. The star magnolia trees have blooms again, but the flowers have come back as sharp as glass; they'll prick your fingers if you dare to pick them. The moths that were once white are now black as coal; white moths only exist as a memory. The deer have turned the color of ashes. The doves that were blinded by the flames have fledglings that are sightless from the day they are born, as if their parents' trauma has been bred into their bones.

In town there are rumors that some of us have also been altered in deep, strange ways. The Enchanted — those said to be witches — are those who stood outside for too long while the cinders rained down, or looked at the sun as it gleamed, or drank from the river when it was thick with toxins. People believe in black magic even when there is none. They assume that whatever is different is dangerous — a snake on the road, a toad in the well. They think that my dear neighbor is one of the Enchanted because she lives alone and seeks no one's counsel or love. Aurora and I used to call her a witch and throw apples at her door, but she's just very old, and wiser than most.

There are those who swear that the stones in my neighbor's field can speak and tell the future. They say she is one of the Enchanted, along with a woman who can fly when the moon is full, another who can change her looks the way a chameleon might — beautiful one day, terrifying the next — and yet another who can swim beneath the water, with gills on her neck like a fish.

Of the fifth, they say only that she is a true believer, although in what or in whom, no one seems sure.

There is truth in the notion that we need magic these days.

Certainly we need protection. The people who destroyed the city travel along the river under cover of night, trying to undermine whatever any village may try to repair. We hear explosions while we are asleep in our beds. Our enemies like the way our world is now, without the things they call *the inventions of doom*. On the darkest nights, their soldiers kidnap women who wander off to look for night-flowering quince. They drag away any man who dares to disagree with their way of life, depositing him in a prison from which, it is whispered, no one ever escapes.

These soldiers do not look evil when you come upon them, riding their beautiful black horses.

They have open, handsome faces. They will offer you food, advice, their side of the story. Some of our own people have joined with them, including my schoolmates who had formed the Forgetting Society at a shack in the woods, all of them orphans, all of them lost. My old schoolmates tried to erase their pain with drugs and drink. When they discovered that wasn't possible, despair overcame them. Some ran away or drowned themselves. Some vanished, as my friend Heather had, though I had tried to convince her that even if she was an orphan, she still belonged. A few young people from our village joined the Horde in exchange for a meal, yearning for something to believe in, desperate enough to accept the Horde's philosophy of destruction. They were willing to adhere to one of the Horde's strictest rules.

Should they ever happen upon a book, they were to tear up the pages, soak them with precious kerosene, and let them burn.

In town, our people lock their doors when dusk falls. They board up their windows, blow out the candles. After they say their prayers, they go to sleep with knives beneath their pillows. They never step outside to see the white sliver of the moon in the sky. They haven't noticed that the ash, which obscured the night skies for so long, has drifted away and that we can once again see the stars.

I still work in my garden at night. My mother taught me the best time to harvest is when the moon is in the center of the sky. The best time to plant is when it wanes. I have Onion to protect me. He would bark to alert me if anyone tried to climb the fence that surrounds my garden. The wooden pickets are adorned with glass bottles that sing when the wind blows through. The glass would shatter if anyone dared to sneak in. Not that anyone would. I am far away in the woods. I'm just Green, who can make any garden grow.

Green, who writes stories. Green, who has managed to go on alone.

I've never minded the dark. I can disappear into it, with my green-tattooed skin, my long black hair. I disappear into my stories the very same way. I lose myself inside the ink. I have written about the way the light fell across my mother's face as she told me good-bye, the song my father whistled, the last time Aurora waved to me on that bright morning.

I'm afraid that soon enough there won't be anything more to tell.

There is only one story I want to get to the end of now.

Will he come back to me?

Will I want him if he does?

Today I have my ink and the pen I fashioned from a sharpened hawk feather. I set off with Onion. I have decided to go looking for the Enchanted — if they exist. I want more than just the stories that come to my kitchen, or the ones that follow me down the streets of my town. I want the difficult stories, the ones that aren't easy to believe, the twisted ones, the sorrowful ones, the ones that need telling most of all.

I wear my long green dress for the journey. My feet are bare. I have paper that I specially invented for my neighbor, the one they call a witch. It's made of nettles and shards of rocks. Her paper is heavy. It shimmers like starlight.

Onion runs ahead through the woods. We come upon the three stacks of stones I made to remember and honor my family. A memorial to those I loved and love still. White and silver and black. Moonstones and sunstones and midnight-black stones.

I stop and say what I think is a prayer. I ask for a blessing. I ask to always remember. Then I try to catch up to Onion.

We reach the field of rocks between the woods and my neighbor's house. These are the stones people say can tell a person's future. Although I am no longer caught in the past, the future seems like a ridiculous thing to me. Try to catch it, hold it in your hand. It disappears every time.

I go to knock on my neighbor's door. We have watched over each other in every way we can ever since the city burned down. I deliver food from my garden, and she's brought me closer to understanding the person that I've become. If that's the trick of a witch, then perhaps she is one after all. She was the only person who could help me to see that despite all my loss, I was still myself, still Green at the core.

Are you sure you want to come in? she says, as if there might be something dangerous inside. It's funny, really. I've been here to visit a hundred times. I have spent many Sundays in her parlor. I've washed her windows, brought baskets of yellow and red tomatoes, eaten a birthday cake she baked just for me.

Of course. I laugh. *I want to write down your story.*

Once you write it, you'll know it, she warns me.

I come inside and sit at her table. I write down everything she tells me. How she had been a beautiful young girl whose true love went to war, how she closed down her heart when he never returned. She had watched the world from her window, going no farther than her own stony field. Then one day she woke up and she was old. She had thrown her life away with her mourning. She hadn't known how to go on. She confided that on the burning day, she'd stood unprotected in the firestorm and let the cinders rain down on her. She thought the world was ending and she was ready to have her life be over as well. But it didn't end, and now she can see the future in the rocks in her field. I laugh because I don't believe her.

My neighbor laughs right back. *You think a stone can't save you?*

A year ago, stones had fallen when marauders from the Forgetting Shack tried to take everything in my garden. Someone had come to my rescue, scaring the thieves away. I knew it was my neighbor who had saved me then. But I'd never known why. Now she tells me that she saw herself in me.

She saw past my tattoos to the grief I was trying to cover with ink. She didn't want me to waste my life the way she had wasted so much of hers.

Perhaps she'll help me once more.

I follow her into the field. My sister and I often came here to gather apples. Now there is only brown grass and rocks. After a time, I lean down and pick up a stone. It's green. It seems like mine.

Tell me my future, I say, not thinking she can.

What you are able to dream you are able to grow, she says to me. *If you don't believe in it, it can never happen.*

She tells me to look, insisting my future is within the stone. When I look carefully, I see a leaf inside the rock.

Nothing grows in stone, I say to my. neighbor. *It's impossible.*

Just watch, she insists.

We sit there for a long time, until at last the moon rises. Every stone in the field becomes a tree. Every tree is growing taller. I fall asleep because I'm certain I must already be dreaming. But in the morning, when I open my eyes, I'm surrounded by a forest.

In one hand I hold the stone with a leaf inside. In the other there is a leaf with a stone weighing it down.

I take them with me when I go.

Ever since that visit I walk along the river. I think about the way things change, about leaves and stones, about the future. I can't stop myself from wondering about these matters even though I know it's a foolish thing to do. I had taught myself to live in the moment, go day by day, forget about wanting more for myself. But my neighbor had made me wonder what might happen next.

Perhaps that is a kind of witchery, a spell she has cast.

One day as I walk along, I hear something in the distance. I kneel and listen to the earth. Something is brewing. It sounds like a windstorm underground, a change that is to come.

Onion darts off into the woods. I follow, calling. He stops by a cliff of craggy rock. I kneel and listen to the ground again. What I hear now is an echo, like my garden growing, but noisier. It's the sound of machines, something I haven't heard all this past year.

I tie Onion to a tree, tell him to hush, then creep toward the cliff. There is a cave right in front of me. If a bear is inside, so be it. If a monster is there, there's nothing I can do. I'll never know if I don't go to see.

I keep on. It should be dark inside, but it's bright, as if a thousand candles are burning.

There are pieces of metal scattered around: cogs, wheels, nails, wires. Generators and lanterns glow. I realize only one person could have managed all this. I have entered the workshop of the Finder. I feel awed that someone has gathered together so much of our past. His back is to me as he works, but when he hears me he turns, an arrow in a bow aimed at my heart.

Despite the threat, I laugh when I see him. He's only a boy. Thirteen at most. He looks familiar. He's probably someone who was several grades behind me in school. A boy to whom I never paid much attention. Someone my sister might have known.

No one is allowed here, he tells me.

For someone so young, he's very sure of himself. The king of the junkyard, of all that was lost.

I recognize him then. He'd been a nervous boy, a prize student, too shy to speak in front of anyone. His sister had done all his talking for him, as mine had once done for me.

His sister was Heather Jones. The girl I'd tried and failed to save.

I know you, I say. *You're Troy Jones.*

He still has the arrow pointed at me. But he seems hesitant once I call him by name. Still, a boy playing with a dangerous toy can be dangerous himself.

I knew your sister, I say. *Heather was my friend.*

Now that he realizes who I am, he puts down the bow. *I've heard about you. You're the one who writes stories. I made something for you. I thought you might come by someday. You look for stories the way I look for machine parts.*

He's rebuilt a typewriter for me. It's made of mismatched pieces, with clackety old keys and leather straps I can use to carry it like a backpack. It is the best gift anyone has ever given me.

Why would you do this? I want to know.

There's something I can't find, Troy Jones admits. *Something I need from you.*

Impossible. I've heard you can find anything.

He shakes his head sadly. *I can't find Heather.*

He had only one sister, as had I. He's an orphan now, too.

I sit him down and tell him his sister has disappeared. When I'd gone to look for her, all that had remained were a few scraps of a blue dress near a fire pit. I'd given her the dress; it had belonged to my mother and it had been beautiful. I tell Troy that Heather is gone and there is no sense in searching for her.

Troy insists I'm wrong. He has a camera, the only one in our village. He found packets of film that raise images as if by magic. He has taken some snapshots he wants me to see. They're grainy and dark but I manage to make out the images. There is my friend Heather — just a fleeting glimpse, but Heather all the same. She is caught in the stoptime of the camera as one of the Horde lifts her onto his black horse. The dress Heather wears is a ragged blue. It's the dress my mother had worn to dances when the world was different. Now, like a miracle, it appears once more.

I ran after them, but I couldn't catch up, Troy tells me. *People say one of the Enchanted can tell you how to find your heart's desire. I know you've set out to collect their stories. All I want is to know where my sister is now. I want you to collect that for me.*

I've heard the same idle gossip. One of the Enchanted is said to see the future, one can see disaster, one can see true love, one can save you, one was a believer. People guess which among them could grant you your heart's desire. It has become a game children chant when they jump rope.

Stone, Sky, Rose, River, Earth.
Let me know just what I'm worth.
Tell me where my true love can be found.
In the sky, the flowers, the river, or deep in the ground.

I've tried every other way to find Heather. Troy's voice is insistent. *Now I need you.*

Why me? I want to know.

Because the Enchanted will talk to you. They'll tell you their stories.

I thought that what you lost you could never get back. I thought I knew the end of most stories. But I was wrong.

I spy a magnifying glass on the worktable. I grab it, then take a closer look at the photograph. My hands are shaking. The half of my tattooed heart feels the way it had when the first needle went in. Like ice. Like heat. As though it had begun beating.

I thought I recognized the denim jacket worn by one of the Horde riders.

Now, upon a closer look, I do.

It's the person whose story I want most of all, the boy who appeared in my garden, the one who'd gone in search of his family, only to disappear.

Diamond.

The boy I loved.

I don't turn on the lantern that night. I sit alone in my house, in the darkness, my sister's dog beneath the table. I can hear crickets in the garden. I hear moths at the windowpanes. Troy Jones asked for my help because he believes I can hear what no one else can. A cry in the distance. A heart that beats when all else is still. He is convinced that people will tell me their stories, and in those stories we'll find what we're looking for. Lies, after all, can be unearthed in many places. But the truth is much harder to decipher, on this we agree.

There's only one way to know if he's right.

I must find out for myself.

Sky
Witch

This is what I learned

What you see, you can understand.

Someone once told me this, but I laughed
out loud.

I said I had seen smoke and ashes and death
and I didn't understand any of it. I had seen love
as well, and that had turned out to be the biggest
mystery of all.

But I had looked at the outside of things, not
at the true, ever-changing heart. Look at a cloud

and see how it becomes a swan, a rose, a lantern, a lion. That is the only way to understand that all clouds change.

Not a single one can ever stay the same.

That doesn't mean it's not still a cloud.

The Enchanted never allow themselves to be known. They don't wish to be made into goddesses or demons. They are merely women who have suffered. They want to be left alone. They know what happens to witches in this world. Every little girl does.

Because they won't reveal themselves or deny their existence, people tell lies. But a lie is not a story, it's simply a lie. Lies become bigger, and fatter, and meaner every time they're told. They eat air and inflate with each piece of gossip. They feel real, but when you touch them, they pop like a bubble. There's nothing inside.

People have begun to say that the Enchanted steal children and keep them in cages. They cast spells in which dogs become men and men become dogs. They turn women into birds, fish, stones, thorns, hedges, monsters.

The townspeople whisper that the witch who can fly sleeps in a nest; she lays eggs and has feathers and talons. They say she knows things a flesh-and-blood woman has no business knowing. She knows your thoughts, your deepest despair, your brightest hope. She can call you by your given name even though she's never seen you before. If you aren't careful, she gets inside your mind. She understands you better than you understand yourself, seeing through to your truest self, whether you like it or not.

Hers is the first story I want to hear.

I start down the road with Onion and a basket of food, the typewriter strapped to my back. The packet of paper I made is stored in a mesh bag I use for drying herbs and sometimes for carrying Onion when he grows tired. I walk for miles under a cloudless sky. I like the feel of the road under my feet, I like the fresh air, but I don't like my own fears. What if the whispers are true? What if the last thing a witch wants is to tell her own story?

Clouds begin to appear in the east as if to echo my cloudy thoughts. They form a tower, a heart, a ring, a bird without wings.

Diamond left me to find his mother and his people. But what if his people are our enemies? What if I hadn't seen him for who he really was? What if our love is something I'd only imagined, yearned for, invented out of air?

My journey takes a day and a night. At last, I see the high tower where the Sky Witch lives. It was once a fire tower. A fire marshal watched over our valley from this vantage point, on the lookout for the signs of smoke. But there is no longer a fire brigade. All our firemen went to the city on the day of the disaster, and they never returned. They crossed the bridge in a desperate attempt to save whoever might be left, but the flames leapt higher and the bridge collapsed behind them.

These men can't be replaced. Not ever.

Now if something is set on fire, our people simply stand and watch it burn.

I pop Onion into the mesh bag, then begin up the rickety ladder. I climb higher and higher, past the tops of the trees, right through a cloud. It's so high I don't dare to look down. I'm breathless, afraid I might fall. But I keep on. I'm at the point where going forward is easier than going back.

I don't stop until I see her. Of course she knew I was coming. She probably knew before I did. She has set out a bowl of water for Onion and a pot of tea made of berries and herbs for me. The tea is blue, hot and salty, like tears. The first sip is so bitter I nearly choke.

You'll get used to the taste, she tells me. And true enough, I do.

The woman who lives in the tower, the one

people swear has feathers and claws, was once the mother of six children. Now she is all alone in a nest made of twigs on the highest platform of the fire tower. The air here is cold and thin and clear. The wind makes you shiver, the sun makes you burn.

The woman in the tower has hair that is knotted with blue feathers; her dress is woven from the down of blue jays. When she sings, the air fills with birds of every variety. Orioles, mockingbirds, nightingales, kestrels — varieties I haven't seen since the city burned down. There are hummingbirds, herons, snowy owls, even parakeets and canaries that have escaped from their cages.

I spy a hawk, one I saved after the fire. He's perched on the roof of the tower — a guard keeping watch over our valley. I had cared for his burns with my mother's lotions and salves. I nursed him back to health and watched him fly away when he was healed.

He looks beautiful here, so high above the world, so at home in the sky.

I'm so happy to see him.

When I tell the woman who lives in the tower I've come to write down her story, she doesn't seem surprised. She doesn't shout or insist I leave as I feared she might. Troy Jones was right. She wants to tell me her story. She actually seems impatient, as if she has been waiting to reveal it for a long time. She speaks so quickly it's not easy to keep up with her. It's like trying to type the wind. She has cried so many tears over the past year that the leaves on the trees beneath the tower have all turned blue. It looks as if there is only sky below us, so vast and endless we can never get back to the ground.

I feel dizzy, but I keep writing. I am still Green, the one who will listen to your story. Green, the searcher. Green, looking for my heart's desire.

The woman in the tower hasn't spoken much since the disaster. At first her words sound like birdsongs, but after a while I understand. She had been asleep with her children when the accident happened, all of them safe and napping in their beds, nestled in a house on the hill. Her husband had been one of the firemen who raced across the bridge before it fell. His name was Jack Bird. Her husband's name sounds like a song in her mouth. She cannot measure his courage.

But can you measure someone's love? I want to know.

You think you can measure love?

She's kind not to laugh at me. I must seem a fool, a girl named Green who doesn't yet understand the world.

No scale would be strong enough, she tells me. *It would break to pieces under the weight.*

On that terrible day, the firestorm ripped through her house in a blinding light. When she opened her eyes, she was alone. Her children had been turned into piles of ash. Her house was destroyed, but she stayed, unprotected from the fallout, the rain, the torrents of leaves, the moths and bats. She slept under a sky that was black at noon. She couldn't leave her children even though people insisted they were no longer there. A group of kindhearted women from town came to comfort her, but she wouldn't even look at them, let alone allow herself to be brought into the village.

Then one day the wind rose up, and the piles of ash that had been her children rose up as well, into the sky, higher and higher. She ran after them, desperate, trying her best to catch up. She went through the woods, past the river, along the road, until she came to this place. She has been here ever since, watching out over the country-side, exactly as her husband, Jack Bird, had done when he was the fire marshal, before he raced into the city on that burning day.

All her life she had been happy but foolish, she tells me. She had been too busy with the small details of her own life to appreciate what she had. She couldn't even remember if she'd kissed her husband good-bye on that last day, or if she had sung her children to sleep before she tucked them in for their naps.

Now she keeps watch over our valley with the help of the hawk. Lately, her eyes have been watering. There has been smoke. The Horde is going from town to town with their torches. They're coming closer to our village.

From up here I see everything, the woman in the tower tells me.

She is nothing like the gossips suggested, not a birdwoman with talons and a beak, squawking and wheeling across the sky. Just the mother of lost children with feathers in her hair.

What you see, you can understand, she says.

I don't believe that, I tell her. I still can't make sense of anything I've seen.

Look at it from the inside, she tells me.

On that terrible day, she had gazed up into the sky for too long, staring straight into the burning black sun. She had lost her children and her brave husband. It seemed she had nothing more to lose, but she had.

Only then do I realize that her eyes are milky. She has lost her sight. She's a blind woman keeping watch over our village, our valley, our lives. Still, her lack of vision doesn't keep her from knowing what our future might bring.

I can tell they're coming closer because of the birds, she tells me.

She hands me a single blue feather, which I slip into my pocket alongside the stone that contains a leaf.

Every day more flocks of birds come to our valley, she says.

They're being chased out of the woods by the fires soldiers from the Horde are setting in villages along the river. Each time the attackers ride in on their black horses, more people are captured and brought to their prison.

Can you grant a heart's desire? I ask. I'm asking as

much for myself as I am for Troy Jones. *Can you find someone who's been lost?*

Someone may be able to, but it's not me, she says sadly. *I can only tell you about what I lost. I can only tell you my story.*

When I write her story, I record the names of all her children and everything they had loved. Jonah had loved apples and William had loved trucks. Sarah had loved books and Melinda had loved hopping about in the rain and Loren had loved rolling in the grass. The littlest of all, the baby named Sam, had loved waking up in the morning and seeing the color of the sky. The paper I use for her has feathers mixed in. The color is a pure pale blue. It looks like spirit paper, cloudy, sky-tinged, as though it's been saturated with tears.

By the time the story is told, it's late and I've grown tired. The woman in the sky lets me stay overnight in the tower. I'm not bothered by the height anymore. All night the wind blows and the woman who lost her children keeps watch. She never sleeps. She is beyond sleep, she confides, day and night are one and the same. But I sleep deeply for the first time in a very long time. I don't worry that my garden may be growing over the windows and doors. That night I dream of six stars in the sky and six birds in a nest. I dream about a baby who loved gardens and green living things.

When I wake just before dawn, I'm alone, the dog sleeping at my feet, the clouds all around me. The woman with no children is gone. I notice there is blue fabric woven into the nest.

I think of Heather Jones.

I think of Diamond.

I try to see with my heart and not only with my eyes. I gaze out and try to look beyond what's right in front of me.

There are flocks of birds in the distance. The blind doves that often nest in my garden are reeling through the air. Among them is one blue-bird flying straight into the wind, higher than all the rest. Her shape is the form of a woman. She perches on the roofs of houses in our village to sing children to sleep with lullabies. She keeps watch all night long, making certain no one's house burns down in the dark and no one else's children are lost.

When the morning breaks open into bands of clear light, I can see farther than I ever have before, all the way along the river. This tower is the highest point for miles around, and the landscape is like a quilt stretched out before me. Villages and fields and woods are a hodgepodge of yellow and green. I see windmills and roads and roses and houses. In the distance, on the other side of the river, lies the city. From here it still looks beautiful, as it did when it was made out of silver and gold.

Then I notice something I've never seen before. In the center of the river there is an island where an old prison once stood. The prison is well hidden by shrubs and vines. You can't see it from our village, only from up here in the sky. This is where the Horde takes men who won't give up the future, and women who refuse to step back into a time when they had no words and no rights.

From this distance the prison looks like a castle. Smoke spirals from the watchtowers. Skulls are nailed to the cornice stones. I spy a flag of ragged blue fabric waving in one window. To me it looks like a flag made of tears.

The flag disappears after only a moment, but I have seen it. A sign from Heather Jones. I'm sure of it. But where is the person I had loved, the boy who gave me my heart, then broke it in two?

Where is Diamond?

I walk home thinking about things I thought I was done with. Love, loyalty, lies. It rains and the rain is green. When I reach my gate, I see that my garden has grown even taller. I cut a path through the twisted wisteria, the blood red roses, the beans on vines that reach all the way to the chimney top.

After I feed Onion, I work on the books I've written, sewing the pages together. I use vines as my thread, thorns as my needles. I have a bookcase full of stories now. The baker's story smells like cinnamon. The scientist's story has the scent of grass. My teacher's tale of the books she loved has stray words that fall out when I turn the pages. *Heath* and *desire* and *moors.* My neighbor with the field of stones has a book so heavy it nearly breaks the shelf in two.

When the book for the woman who lost her children is done, it's so light I have to tie it to the floor to stop it from rising up to the ceiling.

That week when I trek into town with my wheelbarrow of vegetables, Onion follows along, barking at everyone we pass. I notice that the children in the village are singing the lullaby, the one they'd heard in their dreams. I think about the Enchanted. I wonder why it is that those who are the most wounded can often see what others cannot.

More than ever I want their stories on my bookcase.

I want them to last.

The Finder soon comes to see me. I'm easy to locate. You don't need much talent to find me. I'm planting red snap peas in my garden on a dark night. Because I'm still thinking about Diamond, the beans are all turning red. When people in the village eat them, they'll dream of kisses. They'll want to go out looking for love.

The moon is hidden behind clouds, but the weather is warm. It's late spring. Soon enough I'll be turning seventeen. Somehow that seems old to me. So much has happened. So much is gone. I'm lonely in a way I don't understand. I feel like one of the black moths flitting around a lantern, looking for the moon and finding only a false light, burning its wings in the process.

When the Finder appears, Onion doesn't growl. Troy Jones wants to know if I found the witch who can grant a heart's desire. I shake my head.

I tell him what I saw from the tower, the island prison in the center of the river. The skulls and the smoke and the blue flag.

I had believed that Heather had fallen asleep near the fire. I thought she'd been burned to ashes. I presumed I knew her story, but I'd been wrong. Now I wonder if perhaps you can't know the end of something until you get there.

We go inside and have a meal of tomato soup and nettle bread. I serve Troy a slice of cake made from pumpkin seeds and chestnut flour. It's my mother's recipe, so of course it's delicious. He wolfs down the cake, then politely asks for more. I know he's thinking about everything I've told him, and thinking makes him hungry. He's only a boy, after all, still growing. In time he will be tall — six feet tall, maybe more.

As he eats the pumpkin cake, Troy tells me he became the Finder by accident. When he began to search for his sister, he discovered so many other things our village needed. He reminds me that his father had been a carpenter. Troy himself was always a tinkerer by nature. He's good at puzzles and can easily put most contraptions together. He tells me this is why he has decided to go to the prison. If his sister is there, he's certain he can help her escape.

I'm not so certain. Surely, he will be seen as a threat. If he goes to the prison in search of Heather, he will most likely be caught and arrested, perhaps locked up for years. But a girl who is a mere weed can slip in and out of the dark. That's what's needed. Someone no one will notice. Someone who can find Heather.

Someone like me.

I convince Troy, and yet I still have doubts. I spied the blue flag in the prison window, but I don't have faith in my own vision. Perhaps it was only a shadow, a cloud, a blue jay in the far distance. Who am I to leave my garden and go in search of anything? For that you need a believer, and that isn't me. You need someone who is certain the future is a possibility, who is convinced that lost things can be found.

I wish my mother, who always offered such good advice, was here to tell me what to do. I wish my father, who was always so strong, could go and kick down the prison gates. I wish my sister, with her open nature, could remind me to follow my own heart, a heart I'm not even sure I have anymore.

Troy insists he can convince me there is something for me to find. *All you need do is open your eyes and look,* he tells me. He brings a small wooden box out of his pocket, the kind that is often tied to the leg of a dove to send messages into the city.

It must have fallen off one of the doves nesting in your

tree. It was right in your garden but you didn't see it, Troy tells me.

I probably walked past it scores of times. But I never once spied it there in the grass.

I slide open the cover of the little wooden message box. Inside there is a tiny painting. I feel a tightness in my chest. Diamond had been a painter. Even when he couldn't speak, he could show me how he felt through his paintings.

When I unroll the scrap of canvas, I see my own face. But the face is beautiful. I know I don't look like that. Except, perhaps, in the eyes of someone who loves me.

On the back of the painting, half a heart has been painted in red.

The half he took with him when he left.

Look at the mark on the box, Troy tells me.

It's a prison stamp. A small black skull, like the ones nailed to the tower, the ones I'd seen from my perch in the sky.

Is Diamond a prisoner or a guard? Is he my worst enemy or still my beloved? Can I find anything, or simply lose more?

I must have spoken aloud. I must need an answer. The Finder is happy to oblige.

That's for you to find out, Troy Jones says.

We leave the next morning.

Rose
Witch

This is what I hoped

What you look for, you may find.

Someone promised me this, but I shook my head.

I insisted that what was lost was gone forever.
I believed that *searcher* was simply another name
for *fool*.

I had made a life for myself in the village. I
had gone on despite my sorrow, difficult as that
was. It should have been enough to wake up every
day, to see the roses in my garden, to know I was

alive. Surely, wanting more would only bring more despair.

But desire can drive you for miles. It can lead you in ways you never would have imagined. A map can be written in ashes, earth, water, air. Take a step and keep walking. Don't be afraid to look back.

In the end, every path you choose takes you closer to what you've been searching for all along.

Troy and I set off together. I tell him that I've heard that the Rose Witch likes gifts. People say she's vain and silly, a greedy, foolish woman. But no one can agree on a description. How she looks seems to depend on the viewer. The grocery owner's wife, who had once delivered food to her cottage, told me that the woman who lived there was so ugly she had run away without being paid, something I had difficulty believing.

On the other hand, Uncle Tim vows she is the most beautiful woman he's ever seen. He was wandering through a meadow with his dogs when he spied her. He swore her long hair was the color of roses. But of course he had been far away, and the witch disappeared when she noticed him, her own dog at her heels.

The children who play in the town square say that whenever they leave flowers beside her road, she repays them by setting out little cakes that taste like pistachio or almond. If you bring her roses, she gives out special chocolates, the kind we never see anymore, with cherry-red centers.

The children don't believe she is a witch at all.

The toll-taker at the bridge stopped by one day just to give me his opinion. He was shy, and I waited for him to tell me what he thought. He saw the witch in his own way. The Rose Witch could be a hundred different women with a hundred different faces, if what everyone says is true.

The toll-taker told me the Rose Witch was so lovely that she would entrance men on their way to the bridge. He swore he'd seen it time and again — but of course from a distance, like all the rest. Men would give up everything for her and follow her home. Only then did she reveal herself to be a monster. I noticed the toll-taker's glasses were broken. He had to squint when he looked across the table to see my face. I wondered if he saw monsters where there were none. If everyone's inner vision decided who the Rose Witch was.

As for me, I believe that even a monster has a story to tell, so I bring along extra paper. I've used rose water so that the pages are tinged with flecks of crimson. I added a handful of red petals. For some reason this paper made me cry when I cut it into sheets. It was as though I had mixed up true love without even trying. Bees hovered over the kettle, as if there was honey inside. There hadn't been bees in our part of the world for a long time. I took their return as a sign of good luck.

On our journey I carry my typewriter on my back. I am bringing an armful of my most beautiful roses, some of them as big as cabbages. They are the best things I have to offer. Onion follows and Troy Jones leads the way.

We stop to pay our respects at the stone monuments I built for my family. We stand quietly in the middle of the woods and bow our heads. I wonder if you ever miss people any less. I would trade anything to have one word from my mother, one hug from my father, one day to run through the fields with my sister.

Onion is well behaved for once, but as soon as we leave the stacks of stones and head for the road, he races out in front, flushing rabbits from their hiding places, although he's never quick enough to catch one.

The bees follow along, drawn by the huge red roses I'm holding. In no time there is a stream of bees humming like mad. When we can see the bridge, I feel a lump in my throat. I still don't think I will ever walk across it. I look at it, spanning the river, and all I can remember is that day. I remember I was the selfish girl who stayed home. I still wake up every morning though the others are gone. I still bleed. I breathe. I alone have gone on.

There is still very little traffic in and out of the city, perhaps one traveler a day. When the toll-taker spies us, he waves from his booth. We are too far away for him to see clearly, and I don't think he recognizes us. From this distance, how can he tell who is a monster and who is beautiful?

I stick out my tongue to test him, but the toll-taker just keeps waving, friendly as ever. Troy and I laugh. Clearly, that man can't see a thing.

There is the road off to the side, one you might walk right by if you weren't searching for something. We stop laughing. The witch's road is lined with dead things. Brambles. Black trees. Stalks of belladonna and hazel and thorn apple. Skeletons of mice and raccoons and rabbits that were burned alive. These fields suffered from some of the worst of the fires. After all this time, the soil is still hot. I am grateful I decided to wear my boots. I put Onion into the mesh bag and carry him so he won't burn his paws.

I thought the bees would flee, but they follow along. Troy Jones has brought a sword. Just in case. But instead of enemies we have found brambles. Troy looks like a boy playing at war. If our world hadn't been changed, that's what he might be. But now he is the Finder. He puts the sword to good use. He cuts down all the dead growth. When he's done, I lean down and put my hands into the earth. I can feel the beginning of something. As we walk on, the vines unfold behind us. The witch hazel blooms with yellow flowers. Meadowlarks crisscross the sky. We can barely hear each other over the thrumming of the bees. I can't make out what Troy says to me. He looks worried. He points to the house at the end of the path.

There is a woman waiting for us in her doorway.

Maybe we should go back, Troy Jones says now.

All this talk of witches has made him nervous. He's a thirteen-year-old boy who'd been on his own since the day of the fire. Of course he's mistrustful. Anyone would be. But I'm not about to turn away now. I have spied a dog on the porch, a big white greyhound, one I had rescued after the fire. I'd helped to heal her burned paws, then set her free to find her home. I'd called her Ghost because she had appeared in the woods one day, so quiet she was like mist drifting between the trees. Now she runs to us, then leaps to greet me.

I'm so happy to see her.

Come on, then, the woman in the doorway calls when she sees that her dog welcomes us. *Unless you're afraid.*

From this distance she might be beautiful or she might be a monster. I understand all the confusion now. Truly, it's impossible to tell. You have to look from the inside out.

We're here to see you. Whoever you turn out to be, I call back.

This must be the right thing to say, because she waves us on.

As we approach we see that she's just a woman with red hair who had been burned in the fire. Sparks had fallen on her face and left their mark. I present the roses, which she arranges in a vase. She has beautiful hands and a sweet speaking voice.

I explain that we are searching for Troy's sister.

Is there anything else you're searching for? the red-haired woman asks me.

There's something about her that makes me think of true love. The truth slips out before I can stop myself.

There's someone named Diamond, I admit.

She takes us through her back door. A single white rosebush grows there, surrounded by a field of black ashes.

The woman stops me. She puts one hand on my arm.

Before you go any farther you should know one thing: What you look for, you may find.

I had thought there wasn't anything to find behind her house other than a ruined field where nothing could grow. I thought true love was something I had only imagined.

But when I look past the roses I see the island where the prisoners are kept. There are the turrets, there are the skulls. A blue flag hangs in a window, wound through the metal bars. A dozen white doves circle the tower, the same ones that nested in my garden. A trail of white rose trees frames a path that will take us to the riverbank.

It's growing dark. We ask if we can spend the night before we set out on the path of ashes. We still have a long way to go. While Troy sleeps on the couch in the parlor, I set up my typewriter. When I take out the paper I made, I realize it has changed. The rose petals I added have turned from red to white. The paper has become smooth as silk. It smells of rose water and sulfur, a combination that could make anyone cry.

The red-haired woman is ready to tell me her story. The accident happened on her wedding day. She had wanted everything to be perfect, so she told her guests to go ahead into the city. All her family, her friends, the groom.

Don't take too long, her beloved had said.

But she did. She took her time. She wanted the day to last forever. She wanted everything to be just right. She washed her hair with perfumed soap and made her own bouquet with two dozen white roses plucked from the hedge outside her door. Her dress was made of silk — she'd sewn it herself, adding the beads and pearls. She took an iron and lovingly pressed out each wrinkle.

By the time she was ready, she was extremely late. She had to run, her dog at her side. She saw her groom on the bridge, signaling for her to hurry. There was a crowd and she couldn't get through. All of a sudden the bridge wasn't there anymore. There was nothing but fire. Her dress turned red. Her hair turned red. The roses in her hands turned reddest of all, consumed by the flame. Her dog ran off and barked for her to follow. But she wouldn't leave. She wouldn't turn away. She watched the bridge sink into the water. The tears she cried burned themselves into her face, leaving their marks in her skin.

By the time she turned away, everything was gone.

A single petal from the roses I've brought her falls onto the table. It's turned a pure white. I think of my garden in winter. I think of Diamond.

You wanted to know how heavy love is? she says. *So light you can carry it your whole life long.*

Can you grant a heart's desire? I ask her then.

Oh, she says. She seems surprised. She looks at me carefully. *Aren't you Green?*

I nod. That's me. Green, who writes down stories, who still doesn't know the truth about love. Green, who pricks her fingers on roses yet never cries. Green, who is still searching for things she doesn't believe she can ever find.

The woman who had almost been a bride is sadder than ever.

I had hoped you would do that for me, she sighs.

That night I can't sleep. I take Ghost and Onion for a walk. The bees are still in the meadow, still rumbling. Everywhere Troy cut down the brambles, everywhere I'd put my hands into the earth, the plants are growing so fast I can see leaves unfolding in the dark. There are apple trees and stalks of new grass.

I am still Green, who has a talent in the garden. Green, who can make nearly anything bloom. But that doesn't mean I can grant a heart's desire. For me, half a heart is painful enough.

The dogs have run off into the darkness and now I have to search for them. I whistle, but they don't come running back. At last I find them in the campground where Uncle Tim keeps the town's abandoned dogs. There are dozens of them, but I spot Ghost and Onion right away.

Uncle Tim is so lonely that he's grateful for the opportunity to walk me back to the road, his band of strays charging ahead. He tells me stories about his life in the city. He'd been a gardener. He'd found great pleasure in bringing green things to life on city streets, where there would have been only cobblestones and bricks had it not been for him.

When we turn onto the witch's road, Uncle Tim grins. He notices the humming in the fields. He says bees always mean a garden is beginning.

That is a fact, he says. *Gardens are stronger than buildings. They bloom when everything else is gone.*

The red-haired woman is waiting for us. From this distance she looks like a dream. She looks like a photograph taken in the past, trapped behind the meshing of her screen door. She seems uncertain about stepping out. I understand only too well. When you are the sole survivor of anything, do you have the right to be alive? Is the future a betrayal of everyone you ever loved and lost, or is it a way to praise them?

The greyhound and Onion run to the red-haired woman. Uncle Tim's dogs race to her as well, even though several of them are usually standoffish.

That's the beautiful woman I told you about, Tim whispers.

We walk up to the house together and I introduce them. Uncle Tim bows.

At last, he says to the woman inside, delighted to have found her.

I catch the scent of sulfur and burning sugar in the air. I think about the red snap peas I planted in my garden that will taste like kisses.

The red-haired woman opens her door, but she hesitates.

Are you sure you want to come inside? she asks Tim. *Some people say there's a monster in my house.*

He gazes inside. There are the roses in a vase on the table. The Finder is curled up on the couch. Asleep, he seems even younger than his age. A boy who in another world might have been a student, played at war, had a family to watch over him.

Tim laughs. *That's only Troy Jones*, he jokes. *I know him. He's a good boy, not a monster.*

Look at me, the red-haired woman demands. Her voice sounds like heartbreak. *Look carefully.*

With pleasure, Uncle Tim replies. He is younger than I'd first thought. He's so kindhearted no dog has ever barked at him. No child has ever cried in front of him. No bee has ever tried to sting him.

I sit on the floor with the dogs while Tim and the red-haired woman have tea. It's a mixture of rose hips, rose petals, and rose leaves. It must be delicious because they share cup after cup. I don't think they remember that I'm there.

I realize I'm watching the way love begins.

Would you like me to tell your future? the red-haired woman asks Tim.

She sounds uneasy. Perhaps it's a trick question, a way to find out if Uncle Tim thinks the future is a far-off, unreachable country. One in which she doesn't belong.

Why don't you tell me tomorrow when you come to visit me? Tim says before he sets out for home with his dogs. *Come early, so our future together can begin.*

After he leaves, the red-haired woman and I sit out on the porch. We can hear Uncle Tim whistling. We're both thinking about love but we don't discuss it. We just want to think about it in the darkness of the night. Even when we can't hear Tim whistling anymore, we can still hear the bees in the field.

I never thought a map could be made out of roses. I never thought the sound of bees could be so beautiful. In the dark, the marks on the red-haired woman's face look more like white stars than like teardrops or burns.

In the morning when I wake, she's already

gone. She's taken her dog with her, the big white greyhound I'd once set free to find a true home. But she's left an envelope for me on the table.

Inside is a single rose petal.

It's the only map I need.

River Witch

This is who I searched for

Someone once told me that love is an act of will.

I was certain I'd heard wrong.

I thought that love was a river, endless and deep. I thought it merely happened, washing over you like water. It was nothing to search for, nothing to force. I didn't understand that even when we can't control our fate, we alone have the last say in matters of the heart. We can give it freely, even in the worst of times, even when it isn't returned.

The frightened walk away when love is difficult. I know that now. You have to be willing to give everything away. You have to be willing to end up with nothing.

Only then will your heart be whole.

The Finder and I go down to the muddy banks of the river, trekking through the marshes. We pass by toads, snakes, and a strange breed of walking fish that had been forever changed on the day of the accident. But the river is much clearer now. Minnows dart through the shallows. Water lilies appear in our wake, pale green pads with trailing vines and moon-colored flowers. They make me think of my sister, Aurora. I can't help but wonder if it might be true that for every step you take, everyone you've ever loved walks with you.

Two sparrows fly above us. They don't seem the least bit afraid of us. I believe they might be fledglings I rescued after the fire. Sure enough, when I hold out my arm, they light in the palm of my hand. They are so full of life I can feel their hearts beating. Even after they dart off, they circle back to make sure we're still following. They skirt the brambles artfully, utterly comfortable in the air.

I'm so happy to see them.

The sparrows lead us to the edge of the river where there is a cottage made out of an old boat. Troy Jones loves old broken things. He announces that he thinks it's the most beautiful house in the world. Maybe he's right. It certainly is one of a kind. Instead of windows, there are portholes. Instead of a roof, there's a white sail. Every time the wind rises, the house pulls toward the river, as if it yearns to be sailing, as if a house could have its own heart's desire.

A dock trails out into the water. An old woman is there, a lantern beside her. She looks at least a hundred years old. She is the River Witch. Once she had been a fisherman's wife. Now she wears a black shawl.

If she has gills like a fish, the way people

whisper she does, we can't see them. If her skin is made of scales, as the fearful insist, we can't tell. To us she merely looks like a fisherman's wife who has become a widow.

When I ask the River Witch if I can write down her story, she nods. I have added blue fish scales and water lilies to her paper. It shimmers like water, iridescent in the sunlight. But the back of the paper is brown and murky, like the river when it is flooding, when no one can control the way it flows.

Once, the fisherman's wife had only been aware of all she did not have — she wanted a big house, a child, a life in which her husband did not leave her alone for weeks while he sailed down the river to the sea. When the fisherman made his boat into a house so she could travel with him, she had been disappointed. When he brought her bracelets and rings from far-off lands, she was never satisfied. The fisherman was so kindly he could not pass by someone's despair without trying to lend a hand. The fisherman's wife told him that he did too little for her and too much for others. He was always the first to help a stranger, rescue a drowning man, and that is what he did on the day the city burned down. He went out in a rowboat time after time, fishing out those who were swimming away from the fires to save their lives. The last time he went out, he didn't return.

I didn't know his worth, the old woman tells me. *Until it was too late.*

He washed up onshore ten days later, and ever since that time she has not moved from her place on the dock. She has been waiting for a reason to move. She will not leave this place until she can find a way to help others, as her husband once did.

The fisherman's wife invites us to sit beside her. I wonder how she's managed to survive. Why hasn't she starved? She tells me the sparrows bring her bits of fruit and seeds. That is enough to sustain her.

But why do this? I ask.

The fisherman's wife whispers. What she recounts is for my ears alone.

Because love is an act of will. You think it will just happen, but you have to make it so. Even when it's gone wrong. Wait and see. If love doesn't come to you, you have to go find it.

From the dock we can see the prison. There is the blue flag. There are the skulls. So close by, but because of the river between us, so far away. The soldiers of the Horde leave their horses in a pasture on our side of the river and use an old barge to go back and forth to the island.

I recall the photograph of Diamond riding one of those black horses. I feel angry and hurt, then I think of what the fisherman's wife has told me. I will myself to wait, just as the fisherman's wife sits on the dock, waiting.

I will not run away before I know the end of
the story.

Since she has been sitting in the same place for
so long, the fisherman's wife knows more about
the Horde than anyone. She's been watching
patiently the way a fisherman patiently waits for
the biggest fish.

The news she has is grim.

The Horde, she says, *gathers much the way they gathered before burning down the city.*

This time, however, their eyes are on us. The
villagers.

Not again, I think. *Not us.*

I ask how she can be sure. She says she's seen
them stockpiling barrels of gunpowder. She's
overheard soldiers discussing their battle plans.

It makes sense that they would come after us.
We have the Finder. We have generators and
windmills. The future is ahead of us. We have
been starting over.

We have to go back and warn people that the Horde is on the way, Troy says.

No, I say. I feel certain of what we must do next. *We have to stop them.*

The old woman of the river agrees. *While they are gathering for the attack, they have left their prisoners nearly unguarded. You must empty their prison and bring them defeat.*

They are holding at least a hundred prisoners. How can we bring them back to shore? How can we rescue them?

The fisherman's wife surprises us by rising from her place on the dock.

I finally have a reason to move, she tells us. *I'll help you in every way I can.*

She walks slowly along the dock, then up a path made of fish bones. She has been in one place for so long she has to relearn how to walk. We try to help her, but she tells us that some things must be shared and some must be done alone.

When we reach the end of the fish-bone path, she shows us two large wooden levers on the porch of her house. Her husband had been a tinkerer, like Troy. He liked puzzles as much as he liked boats. If the levers are pulled, the house can be pushed into the river. It will be again what it had been before it was their house: a huge sailing ship.

Troy finds the planking the fisherman had once used to slip the boat into the water.

Now I know it was our dreamhouse, the fisherman's wife says. *When we slept together in bed, we dreamed of oceans, starfish, lagoons.*

She takes a fishhook from her pocket. It's small. It looks light, but when she places it in my hand, it is surprisingly heavy.

This is how much love weighs, she tells me. *Nothing if you don't take it when it's offered. Everything if you accept what's given to you.*

We get on board and wait for the tide to rise. The world seems quiet, yet anything seems possible. The fisherman's wife knows how to work the rigging. At last she has a reason to leave her dock, because we need her help. She has a reason to live again.

In the dark we edge toward the island. As we draw close we hear frogs, night birds, waves against the shore. We hear the Horde speaking in a language we don't understand, just as we never understood how they could be so certain that heaven is on their side, that they alone have the right to chart what is a sin. For them, the past is the only marker. The future is nothing but dangerous territory. The death of innocent people is a price they're willing to pay in order to build their vision of heaven on earth.

There is no language that can give a reasonable voice to that.

When I consider the Horde and the prison before us, I'm frightened. Then I think about my sister in the green market in the city just before the fire began, unaware that it was her last day on earth. There were blue skies, sunlight, crowds of people buying lettuce and peas. It should have been just another day, but it wasn't. It should have been me, if I'd gone instead.

I am thinking about Aurora so deeply I can feel her beside me. I'm not as alone as I'd feared. A year has passed, and although I'm different, she is still the same. She will always be my little sister. I close my eyes and will myself to remember. The apples we picked, the songs we sang, the color of her hair, the way she would sleep on the floor with her little dog. I remember it all. If she were with me, my wild, fearless sister would say I have nothing to fear.

Go and don't look back, I hear her say to me.

I am ready.

I take a stone, a feather, a rose petal, a fishhook.

I must leave behind Troy Jones and the fisherman's wife and even little Onion. I have to go alone.

Troy doesn't understand. *I'm going, too,* he insists.

One of us has to return to the village. If I don't make it back, that someone is you.

Troy is about to argue, but the fisherman's wife makes him understand.

Sometimes it takes as much courage to stay behind as it does to go, she tells him.

It's then he realizes that although he has found our way here, it is my place to go onward.

I move forward, into the darkness.

I am Green, used to being alone in the garden. Green, who can make anything grow. I hasten through the reeds and the tall grass as if I were invisible. Just Green, nothing more. The reeds are my armor and my protection. They are my story, the chapters that have been written and those that have yet to be. My feet are bare and I can feel everything growing right up through me, straight into my heart. I need to be hidden. To be one with the earth. I try to become the meadow I'm walking through. I breathe and think like a meadow. I am silent and still like a meadow.

Yet I move forward.

The Horde must think I'm a weed, a vine, nothing worth paying attention to. Then they hear something in the grass. Me. They turn with their rifles.

My heart is pounding inside my chest. I still have a heart, it seems.

I reach into my pocket for the feather the woman who had lost her children gave me. I hold it up, then let go. The wind carries it past the soldiers. They laugh when they spy the feather, relieved. They believe a bird is hiding in the reeds. That and nothing more. But it's me, Green. Green, who has been in the highest tower, who has slept in the clouds, who has seen doves that can find their way even when they can no longer see, who once heard a lullaby that helped even the most frightened children fall asleep.

Even though I feel I am close to Diamond, I'm afraid that once I find him, one of us will have changed too much for the other to recognize. I will myself to remember what we meant to each other. It all comes back to me. That is what the future is. I see that now. The past and the present entwined into one.

There in the meadow I am no longer so alone, as I'd imagined I would be. I think of my mother, who was always so kind to strangers. She left food out at the end of our road for any passing traveler who might be hungry. She did not judge or place herself above anyone else in this world. You could tell her anything and she would listen. When she worked in the kitchen, boiling quince and apples for jam, rolling out pie crust, shelling beans, every move she made was beautiful. In her hands quince and apples became emeralds, rubies, a treasure. She never used recipes. She made it all up, working by instinct. She had her own ways of doing everything. If she were with me now, she'd tell me to trust myself.

Here is the way, I hear her say to me, and when I go on, I find the prison door.

I use the fishhook the fisherman's wife gave me as a key. It works perfectly. One click and I'm in.

It's murky in the corridors. There's no light inside. I find my way to a staircase that leads to the very top of the tower, where I'd seen the blue flag in the window. It's dark, but I hear the murmur of voices. There are no guards posted inside. Only the soldiers out in the grass. Everyone else is getting ready for the battle. But still, the voices continue.

My eyes adjust to the dark. I see people in cages.

I open the lock of each cage with the fishhook key as I pass by. Some of the people are ours, some are theirs, anyone who has disagreed with their methods or spoken out against violence and hate. Anyone who isn't afraid of the future.

It doesn't matter. In our escape we are brothers and sisters. They are all so grateful they want to follow me, offer their help, but I need to go on alone. I whisper where to find the boat.

Run, I tell them. *Don't be afraid. Don't look back.*

A single night isn't long enough for all I have yet to do. I hurry until I am out of breath.

Once more I'm not as alone as I had believed I would be. I think of my father and how hard he worked. Our garden was nothing but brambles at first. He labored all day long and halfway through the nights, chopping back the tangled weeds, turning the soil, carting away stones, building the fences, the arbors, the well, where the water was always so clear and sweet. He told us we were beautiful, whether or not we were. We could have brambles in our hair, mud on our feet, and it wouldn't matter. He told us we didn't have to do anything to please him, except to be ourselves. Once I saw him crying over a deer a hunter had shot and left to die. I was stunned to see my strong father cry. But now if he were here, he would tell me that real strength has no boundaries.

The more you feel, the stronger you are, I hear him say to me.

Heart, soul, treasure, rain, sister, memory, knowledge, hope, will.

I hurry on, two steps at a time.

I am farther than I've ever been from my garden, yet I still feel the garden inside me. Red roses, sweet peas, blackberries, thorns. Lettuce, squash blossom, verbena, rowan, oak. Each plant that grows there has been a gift to me. Each one has made me stronger.

I remember everything about love as I climb the stairs. It's coming back to me now.

How much does love weigh?

As much as a stone, a feather, a rose petal, a leaf.

It's more than we can ever bear and less than

we have the strength to carry. It is invisible. It's right there in front of me. It's made out of stones. It's made out of air.

At last I come to a cell that is so dark, so hidden, the people inside can't see me. When I whisper a greeting, they don't respond. Thinking I'm one of the guards, they back away. I take the single petal given to me by the red-haired woman who still believes in love. I slip it into the cell. As soon as I do, it turns from white to red. Red as my roses, my blood, my heart.

That's when I see his face in the dark, behind the iron bars.

I open the lock with the fishhook. The metal is light in my hands. Once the prisoners are released, they thank me. Though I don't know their language, I know they are offering me a blessing. I nod, but I see only one person among them.

Diamond.

The other prisoners run down the stairs when I direct them to the boat, but he stays where he is.

Diamond.

He's theirs, but he's mine, too. More mine than anything has ever been.

There is no time for anything, but he kisses me.

I sent you a message, he says.

It is the first time I have heard his voice.

This feels like the greatest blessing of all.

His voice has returned. His throat has healed and he's spent his time in prison learning our language.

This is a gift that is meant for me. He tells me that every time he learned a word, it was to say to me.

I admit that it had taken a very long time to get his message, the painting he'd sent to me, but at last I'd received it. Now I understand that the only thing that had kept us apart were my doubts.

He has been with me even though I haven't been beside him. He tells me so and I believe him.

He says he was captured while searching for his family, thrown onto a black horse, taken here. It was here that he found his family: his mother, his sisters, his cousins. All were in prison with him. Now I've freed them and they are with the group hastening toward the boat.

Now we are together at last.

Before he'd left, I had tattooed his skin. Half a rose, half a thorn, half a wing, half a leaf, half a heart. Diamond found ink and pins in prison and completed each one. He added grass and leaves to the ink he used.

As green as apples, he whispers to me. *As green as the love of my life.*

We climb the highest steps of the tower together. There are two guards there, but Diamond surprises them and locks them in an empty cell. Once they are no longer a threat, he whispers that he knows where Heather is. She's had a child, and lately she's been ill. The father of her child was one of the Horde who was supposed to be her guard but who had fallen in love with her. They'd married in a secret ceremony, attended by prisoners from both sides. But when her husband tried to rescue her, he'd been shot by his own people.

Heather's cell has three locks. They must consider her dangerous. They don't want anyone to see what they've done to her, how much they've taken away. Perhaps even they couldn't find a way to explain a reason for such suffering.

The first lock on her cell is gold, the second is silver, the third is made of iron. They're so strong the fishhook key doesn't work. But I still have the stone taken from my neighbor's field in my pocket, the one that was supposed to tell my future, with a leaf growing inside. I crack off the gold lock and then the silver one. My hands are bleeding by now. Diamond wants to help me, but I know this is something I must do alone.

I come to the last lock, the most difficult one to break. When I hit it, the stone from my neighbor's field crumbles into pieces. All that's left is a single green leaf.

But the lock made of iron has opened. We push in the door.

Heather is holding her baby. It's a boy. A scrawny, weak-looking thing. But his eyes are on me, watching.

Heather, I say. I run to be near her.

She's happy to see me but nearly too exhausted to talk.

I didn't give him a name, she whispers. She and the baby are burning with fever. They stare at something in the distance, as if they can only see some far-off place. *I don't know if he'll last long enough to need a name in this world.*

He'll have a wonderful name, I say. *But now we have to hurry. Your brother sent me. He's waiting for you.*

We run down the flights of stairs. Quick and quiet. There are mice, but we pay no attention. There are bats, but they cling to the rafters, wings folded up tight. The stone steps are cold and stained with blood. We don't want to think about that now. The past is over and done. We're running someplace brand-new.

Down from the tower, down from the cells, out the door, into the grass. There is a dark sky tonight. There are a thousand stars up above. We see the Horde and their stockpiles of gunpowder. We see our village on the other side of the river. It looks as though fireflies have flown into the houses. The generators are working. There are lanterns, candles, flickering lights. The world is returning on the other side. Little by little. Bit by bit. Tonight the river is beautiful. Stars reflect in the black water as if they are a thousand boats that have set sail.

We have to hurry, I tell Heather.

Diamond leads us through the tall grass. We're so close to the gathering of the Horde we can feel the ground shake beneath us. We can hear their raised voices. They have spied our boat and now race to bring cannons out from the storehouse. One cannon is quickly set up in the field and positioned toward the river. If fired, it will go right through our sails, our ship, our lives.

Heather pushes her baby into my arms. When he gazes up at me, I see that his eyes are green. He isn't as scrawny as he first appeared.

If anything happens to me, give him a name, Heather tells me.

I couldn't do that, I sputter. Who am I to do so? Only Green. Not an aunt or a sister or even a cousin.

Of course you can. I think Heather smiles. It's difficult to tell in the dark, but I feel her warmth when she embraces me. *That's what a godmother does*, she says.

Everything happens at once. Heather disappears into the meadow before we can stop her. The Horde has left to bring out the rest of the cannons. As we clamor into the boat, we see that Heather is pushing at the cannon in the field, turning it around.

She is much stronger than a sick, feverish woman should be. She's stronger than she looks.

Some people would no sooner put themselves first than a hawk would choose to stay on the ground, or a dog would refuse to run, or a sparrow would decide to make its home in a cage rather than in the open sky. That's not Heather. She thinks only of us.

She lights the fuse of the cannon. She has turned it toward the storehouse where the weapons are kept. The Horde began this battle. Now the death they wished to offer us is aimed right at them.

Some people understand the will to love

someone. They're not about to give up easily. Heather runs back to us as fast as she can. People watching from the boat later say she was flying. Most believed she would never make it, flying or not. The boat is already leaving the shore, the water is between us, the waves, the black water. Still, Diamond and Troy reach out. They grab her and manage to pull her on board.

When the cannon goes off, there is a moment of quiet. Then the storehouse of gunpowder and weapons is hit. There is a roar as everything on the island disappears in an instant. The tower, the cells, the skulls, the blue flag, the heartache, the Horde.

All of it, up in flames.

The people who destroyed our city have been destroyed by their own weapons.

We close our eyes so they won't fill with ashes. We say a blessing, thankful that we are still alive. Some of us speak one language, some speak another. But that doesn't matter anymore.

I sit with Diamond in the dark as we cross the river. He shows me that he finished the heart tattoo I'd begun on his chest.

It is then I can feel something burn inside me.

Without needles, without pins, without any ink at all, my heart is completed now, too, the color of a rose.

Green
Witch

This is what I believe

Someone promised me that we all have our own path and that mine could be found in the garden. She said I was the one who was needed most of all.

It was my mother who said that, but I turned away. I didn't believe a word she said. I thought my garden was the last place that would bring me happiness. I thought I was invisible, on my own, meant to be an outsider. Green, who had no life. Green, with no future.

I had no idea that anyone would ever need me.

Now I understand that my mother was right. Once I'd feared that when I finally wrote about the day my family left for the city, it would be the end of the story, the very last page. But that isn't the way it's turned out. My life is opening like a book. It's growing like a garden without any boundaries.

Heather and Troy and the baby moved into our cottage deep in the woods. There are rooms that hadn't been used for so long the doors had to be pried open. It was a pleasure to clean the windows, to wash the sheets and hang them in the sun, to sweep the floors, to make pies and let them cool on the table, to light candles at dinnertime.

We were all so busy I didn't even notice I had turned seventeen.

All through the summer, my neighbor who lived in the stone field brought Heather nettle soup to help bring back her strength. In autumn, the woman who had lost her children brought a cradle and a high chair. That winter, the red-haired woman who still believed in love came to tell stories and Uncle Tim came with her, bringing a toy dog he made out of acorns and reeds. The next spring, the fisherman's wife who had always sewn fishing nets brought a dozen blankets and hats she had knitted.

Every single one was green.

As it turned out I had a gift for Heather as well. I named her baby. I called him Leaf because he had grown from the love all around him. Leaf, because he liked nothing more than to play in the garden. Leaf, with his green eyes and his quiet disposition. Leaf, who was his mother's heart's desire.

All through the year, as we've worked in the garden together and set right the house, I've often said to Heather, *Aren't you lucky I was sent to find you?*

She always laughs out loud.

I am lucky, she agrees. *But he was the one you were meant to find.*

She means Diamond, and she's right about that. I cannot have enough of him. I love the half of his face that is beautiful and the half that was burned in the fire. Most of all I love the part I can't see. The part deep inside. The boy who learned my language, gave me my heart, never left me even when he was so far away.

Diamond's people have moved into villages up and down the river. They are quiet people, brutalized by the same army that brutalized us. Some of them have moved into the city. They have opened shops, markets, concert halls. We listen to their music. We use their recipes, just as they use ours. Our children are in schools together. Our brothers have fallen in love with their sisters, and theirs with ours. We now speak a language that is half and half. The word for *husband* is ours. The word for *wife* is much more beautiful in their dialect. *Adoreé.* We don't seem very different from one another. We have all lost people we love.

On my eighteenth birthday we decide it's time for a party. Two years have passed since the disaster. Two years since I hid under my bed, refusing to face daylight, no longer believing in anything.

Diamond's family crosses the bridge from the city to come to the celebration. His mother has long black hair like mine. She's shy, but wise and proud of her children. She brings along little treasures for the occasion: strong coffee, apple tarts, sesame candies.

Everyone from town has come to celebrate with us. Onion barks at each and every one. The shopkeeper and his wife. My old teacher, the one who remembers every book she's ever read, brings the orphans, dressed in their best clothes. Uncle Tim and the red-haired woman and the white greyhound come up the road together. The fisherman's wife has fixed a stew. The woman who lost her children sings a birthday song. My dear neighbor from the stony field has brought a green nettle cake that is so tall four strong men have to carry it through the field. When it's set on the picnic table outside, the table teeters under its weight. Everyone who eats a piece of my neighbor's cake cries, moved by the sheer emotion of such a fortunate day. We all look at one another and laugh, then toast each other's good health.

Troy Jones has hung strands of white lights all along the fence. He gives some of the orphaned boys the job of turning the hand-cranked generators. Diamond's mother applauds when she sees the lights. It's so glorious to see, like fireflies in the garden. She leans over and whispers in a language I'm beginning to understand. She wishes us happiness for the rest of our lives.

Diamond gives me the best gift of all. A strand of pearls. They are the pearls my mother had planned to present on my sixteenth birthday, the ones I gave to the shopkeeper's wife in exchange for seeds and a warm jacket for Diamond before he went away. He's traded a season's worth of blueberries and two of his paintings to get them back, but the steep price is more than worth it.

Leaf is in the center of everything, there in his carriage. I notice there are vines growing around the wheels, unfolding by the minute. Little seedlings pop up around him. The lilacs bend in his direction, drawn to him. He is my godchild, so I'm not surprised. I am the Green Witch, after all, the one who can bring your heart's desire. In time I'll teach Leaf everything I learned from my mother. How to bury old boots beside pear trees so they will bear the sweetest fruit. How to spray roses with garlic so aphids will go elsewhere. Before long, Leaf will only have to whisper and the wisteria will bloom. He'll laugh and the tomatoes will ripen overnight.

But I will have to come back to teach him these lessons. Diamond and I are leaving for the city. The world that was so ruined is growing brighter. It shines like silver at night, gold in the sun. The city was always my garden, the people there like flowers, the traffic like a river, the lights of the buildings shining as if they were a hundred white tears. Our stand will be set up in the square where my family was selling vegetables on that day. We have already chosen the space. Troy and Heather and Leaf will bring us lettuce and string beans and baskets of pears. They will tell us stories about the village and we will show them all that's brand-new in the city. At night we will sit at one of the cafés, my sister's little dog, Onion, beside us. We will know how lucky we are.

I am the last person anyone would have expected to believe in the future, but I do. I am not hurrying toward it anymore. I am inside of it. A lifetime, after all, can be spent in a single afternoon. A world can exist in a kiss, a rose, a leaf, a heart. On my window ledge I will always keep three stones: silver for my mother, black for my father, white as the moon for my sister, Aurora.

Late at night, when the marketplace is quiet, when the boy I have always loved is asleep, I will sit in my kitchen with my typewriter. The city is not what it once was — buildings have fallen, parks have burned, trains still don't run. All the same, it's filled with stories, far too many to count. Too many to ever write down in a single lifetime.

Some people say there's nothing but piles of bricks here. They say we'll never be able to build our city again. They say our gardens are gone, but they're wrong.

There are already roses growing outside my door.

Acknowledgments

With gratitude to my brilliant editor, David Levithan, who knew exactly how Green's story should be told; to the amazing Elizabeth Parisi, art director and magician who created Green's world; and to the extraordinary artist, Matt Mahurin, who brought Green to life.

To my readers, thank you for telling me the story wasn't over.